MAFIA BOSS'S FAKE WIFE

A FORCED PROXIMITY DARK MAFIA ROMANCE

RUTHLESS CHICAGO MAFIA KINGS
BOOK FOUR

VIVY SKYS

Copyright © 2025 by VIVY SKYS

All rights reserved.

No part of this book may be reproduced in any form or by any electronic or mechanical means, including information storage and retrieval systems, without written permission from the author, except for the use of brief quotations in a book review.

1

MARCO

I'M DROWNING IN NIECES AND NEPHEWS.

Elio's house is a veritable hive of children. There are babies or young children literally everywhere, including in Elio's arms. We're outside, looking at the carved winter wonderland that Elio had ice sculptors put into place prior to the holiday. The kids, predictably, are still enjoying the many wonders of a backyard filled with ice sculptures that they can walk into.

Elio, Caterina, Sal, and Gia are all chasing each other around the yard. Marisol and Dino, and the twins, are laughing from the top floor of the two-story ice palace that Elio spent an obscene amount of money on.

I stare at Elio, shaking my head.

It would be pretty fucking funny, seeing a man that I once witnessed burn through an entire platoon of bottle girls in a week, covered completely in babies and wearing an apron, but somehow, it's not really that funny.

None of this, in fact, feels like how I wanted it to feel.

I wanted it to feel...

Good.

Instead, looking out at the family holiday gathering, I feel something else entirely.

Nothing.

An emptiness that I know too fucking well, perhaps..

But nothing like the wave of happiness and satisfaction that I had expected.

"Zio Marco!" Luna shouts, her face wide and her eyes a little crazy from eating nothing but straight candy for the past twenty-four hours. "Come play!" She zooms over, her cheeks red with the cold.

I give her the best smile I can muster. "In a minute, stellina."

Luna pouts, a look that's so achingly familiar to me. Caterina looked like that as a kid too, and fuck if it didn't wear me the fuck down.

Time and time again.

I've never been able to say no to my siblings. Not in any way, shape, or form. I might frequently have to navigate my way around many dangers to figure out how to do what's best for them...

But an outright refusal has been something I've been incapable of.

So, looking into my niece's eyes, I give her a wink. I hope to not convey any of my melancholy.

I can't be her favorite zio, after all, if I'm not fun.

"I'll come to play in a minute," I say gently.

Luna sighs, but zips quickly to play with her cousins in the massive ice castle that Elio constructed for all of the cousins. We're in that post-holiday time between Christmas and New Year's where nothing really happens. The kids are all enjoying their gifts, which were an absolute mountain of brightly-wrapped presents mere days ago, and us adults are just snacking on whatever food we can find while drinking our way through Elio's admittedly impressive wine collection.

It's a moment that happens every year. But, considering how much unrest and strife we've been through in the past few years, this one feels special.

This one feels like...

Well. It should feel like a fucking amazing thing. I've worked my ass off to make this day happen. For years, I've been the one pulling the strings to make sure that my siblings can all enjoy this fucking moment.

My siblings are all enjoying the time with their respective families.

Elio and Caterina, with their daughter Luna and their new baby. Dino, my half-brother who has lived his life as the black sheep of our family for so long. Seeing him enjoy his wife, Marisol, and take time out of running the cartel that used to belong to Marisol's father, is wonderful. Their twin daughters, the nieces that I went above and beyond to protect when Dino couldn't, are screaming with laughter as they slide on the ice.

Sal, my second brother and the jack-of-all-trades spymaster for our family, tugs his wife Gia close. Gia is Elio's twin, and arguably one of the most terrifying people on the face of the planet.

Except for now, when she's bouncing their son in her lap, her laughter is clear and brazen in the winter air.

Seeing everyone together is... good. It's everything I've hoped for. Everything I've worked for in the past decade.

It's so different from the De Luca get-togethers when I was a kid. Those felt... hard. Edgy in a way that I don't care to repeat. I'm the oldest sibling, so I remember how tense our family used to be.

How quickly it all fell apart when my grandfather and uncles were sent to jail.

I knew, the second my father told me that I would become the head of the family, that I wouldn't do anything to risk my siblings.

Ever.

In fact, I would dedicate my life to making them happy. The world that we operate in has so little joy, I swore then that I would never take that joy away from my siblings.

I would cultivate it instead.

I told myself that it would all be worth it. That seeing them be happy would be enough, and that I could just fucking suck it up and soak in their joy. That it would be enough for me.

There is joy. It's echoed around me in the joyful shrieks of children and the low hum of conversation. I see it when Sal gives Gia a kiss on the forehead, or when Dino's eyes soften, ever so slightly, when he watches Marisol dance with the girls.

There's plenty of joy.

It just doesn't reach me.

I'm... somewhere else. Distant.

The joy that they feel?

I get none of it.

"If your face gets any more sour, you're going to spoil the wine," Elio mutters behind me.

I roll my eyes. "Fuck off."

"You're lucky Caterina didn't catch you swearing in front of the children," he chides.

I roll my eyes again at that, but move slightly so that I'm following Elio back into the kitchen and in from the cold. My little sister, Elio's wife, is the epitome of kindness. Until, of course, you do something to upset her.

Then, she can raise hell with the best of them, and I have no doubt that Caterina would give me the worst of it if she found out I did, in fact, swear in front of the children.

Inside, I give his apron a meaningful look. "You should wear this to the next business meeting with the Russians. I think it would really put them in their place."

"Fuck you," he says, but there's no fire in the words. Instead, my friend's eyes twinkle with a kind of satisfaction that makes my chest hurt. "You're just jealous that you did not receive such a gift."

"Well I wouldn't, now would I?" I say under my breath.

Elio glances down at where the words "Best Dad Ever" are printed on the canvas. It's a masculine enough looking thing, but the bedazzled words have Caterina and Luna's trademark flair.

Elio's face softens. "I would wear it in front of them with pride, my friend."

The fucking bitterness expands, until it feels like it's pulsing at the edges of my chest. I don't respond to Elio, instead opting to refill my cup.

"Marco," Elio says.

I turn.

His head is tilted sideways, and he studies me. "What?" he asks.

"What do you mean, what?"

"Something is wrong."

"No it isn't," I snap. "Everything is fucking fantastic. The kids had a great fucking Chrtistmas and I remain everyone's favorite uncle, once again."

Elio nods. "This is true. I hate you for getting Luna a full drum set, but she seems to be plenty happy."

That was a particularly inspired idea, and I can't help but smile. "You're welcome."

"And yet,' Elio continues, coming closer to me. "It still seems as though something is...Amiss."

"Nothing is wrong," I grunt.

He looks at me before turning. "Well. Then you'll be ready to tell me how long you plan on sticking around this time."

They could be regular words that any brother-in-law would say to his family.

Or a best friend, to his.

But with Elio, I have known him too long, and I detect the darkness underneath his tone.

For better or worse, Elio may be the only person who understands me and my position.

I open my mouth, ready to say something to him about the fact that I don't feel as fucking content as I've worked to feel, that I'm fucking lost in this sea of family and smiles and happiness, when my eyes drift to the apron.

Best Dad.

It slams into me, then. Elio and I are not alike. At least not in this.

Elio looks at me, his eyes searching mine.

He is a man who has everything he wants.

And I'm one who has nothing.

I shake my head, my smile tight and barely there. "No. I'm fine, Elio."

"You're lying."

I shrug. "If I am, it doesn't change my answer."

Elio studies me for a minute longer, then sighs. "When is the trial?"

Something inside me tightens. "Three weeks."

He nods. "And how do you plan to pull that off?"

I'm not quite sure yet.

I agreed to testify for Interpol, a star witness in a gun running trial against the Irish. My only stipulations, of course, were that my family would not be harmed, and that I would have immunity and protection for my twin nieces. Dino came to me with the secret of their existence many years ago, and I've slowly fed Interpol bits and pieces of information, enough that they continued to watch over Marisol and the two girls.

Until recently.

Recently, the small tidbits of information became a torrent. When Caterina and Elio married, I wanted Caterina to find out if Elio had killed our parents. However, I needed to be sure, so I asked for a bunch of favors with my Interpol handler as well. Compounded with the fact that Dino's now-wife and the mother of his children was kidnapped by her father to be married off...

I had to call in favors.

And favors with Interpol usually mean that you have to return them.

In my case, it's testimony. I'm being forced to show my face in court in three weeks, metaphorically speaking, in order to testify against Liam MacAntyre, and his brother.

Who Elio killed.

Figuring out how to provide evidence to incriminate the Irish, who we now think may have been behind the attack that killed Elio's parents and mine, has been..

Challenging.

Escaping protective custody even more so.

Especially when my jailer had beautiful strawberry-blonde hair and green eyes...

Shut the fuck up, Marco.

I slam the door on thoughts of her before I let them destroy my mood even more.

Elio is still patiently staring at me. I shrug. "So do the kids need to come in off of your giant carved ice palace or what?"

"They have coats," he says with that same curious expression. "They will be fine."

"You're right. They will be. We always make sure they're fine," I snap.

I'm not sure that I meant it to be so harsh.

Elio's eyes narrow. "You have always ensured the safety of the family, Marco. Even if I did not see it. I'm....thankful," he says.

If I wasn't so angry, I'd smile.

Elio struggles just as much as I do when it comes to expressing gratitude.

Instead, I give him a sharp nod. "You're welcome."

"It seems that..." he huffs. "Fine. I'll just state it. Since we are no longer opposed, I would like to discuss with you the possibility of you... reinstating some of your business obligations."

The thought sends a fissure of ice down my spine. "What does that mean?"

Elio nods. "For the most part, De Luca shipping has been absorbed into the Rossi fold. Dino has a handle on the docks, but Gia and Sal have been handling your... end of the business."

He means the unpacking of illegal goods and the distribution. "I know," I mutter.

Being held in witness protection by Interpol, I haven't exactly been around to handle the things I used to.

"It would be nice to bring you back. To the family business," Elio says.

The heavy emphasis on the word 'family' sits in my mind.

Family business.

My whole life, I have been acutely aware of the family business. It has been everything I wanted, everything I aspired to. Everything that I worked, day in and out, to protect. I was the head of the De Luca family very young, when our parents were tragically killed in an explosion following Elio and Caterina's first engagement party.

Elio and Gia's parents were killed as well. For a long time, we both thought that the other was behind the murders.

It drove a rift between us.

Prior to that night, Elio had been my best friend. We're the same age, and went to the same schools. In high school, Elio was a gangly Italian with an accent thicker than mud and a temper that kept people from mocking it.

I enjoyed being his silver-tongued advocate in the world.

The murders of our parents broke us.

The time he spent trying to get back at me through marrying Caterina…

I guess it healed us.

Elio offering to bring me back in is generous. It should make me feel…

something.

The fact that it does not creates a dissonance in my mind that feels like a buzzing beneath my skin.

I mentally shake. "Thank you, Elio. That would be... great," I manage to grit out.

I can tell Elio wants to ask more, but at that time a wail of despair comes from outside. Elio moves, automatically drawn to the doors to the patio, leaving me in the kitchen.

Alone.

When everyone is asleep, I choose to sneak back into the kitchen to fill my glass with Elio's expensive French cognac. Sipping the complex drink, I meander back into the room that I'm staying in.

I grimace.

Even now, looking at the walls in my brother-in-law and former best friend's house, safe and content and happy with my family, I feel that same itch under my skin as I had earlier.

Brought back into the family business.

As though Elio is the family. Elio is the business.

And I am on the outside.

I believe that is what bothers me, but there's another piece of it that feels... strange. Like a puzzle piece that I'm trying to jam into a space that looks like it should fit.

Even though it doesn't.

I wish to feel... at home.

Like I belong.

And not because of Elio's goodwill.

Unbidden, my mind drifts to the last time that I felt like that. When I felt so at home, I almost forgot that I wasn't.

Except...

I suppose I was.

It might be the fucking French alcohol, it might be the loneliness gnawing at me.

But regardless of the cause, I shut my eyes.

And I let myself remember.

A year and a half ago

"You said the water would be cold," I hiss through clenched teeth. "This isn't cold. This is fucking ice."

"Well, aren't you a big tough mafia man then, unable to handle a little Irish water?"

Her voice.

It's always her fucking voice that gets me first.

I've been holed up with Roisin Kennedy, Interpol agent and my handler, for a month and a half. I haven't been able to see my family, have no idea what's happening to Caterina, and I'm...

I should care.

But I don't.

I look over at where Roisin is emerging from the sea, like some kind of goddess. I've tucked myself back onto our blanket, the cold Irish ocean seeping into my bones.

My entire body heats, however, when I observe Roisin coming out of the sea.

She's fucking stunning.

I shouldn't be thinking that about her. She's practically my babysitter, after all.

But fuck.

I do anyway.

She's all muscle, with surprising curves that make my mouth salivate, and there's power in her tiny frame that I know too well. The memory of her taking me down while we were sparring one day, her legs wrapped tightly around my head, makes me hard so fast I have to adjust myself.

Her challenge turns me on.

Because so far, she's put up a good fight in all of our little mock battles…

And it feels so fucking good for me to win them anyway.

"You're going to catch your death of cold," I say to her.

I sound like a fucking nonna, but I can't help it. I don't know what to say to her half the time, and now that I can see the smooth expanse of her bare skin?

It's a miracle I managed any words at all.

Roisin tilts her head back and laughs, droplets cascading down her neck, glowing in the rare sunshine that's blessing us on the beach today. Largely, Ireland is fucking miserably cold and wet.

So when the sun came out today and she told me we should go to the beach, I didn't argue.

Like some kind of fey creature, she hops over the large, smooth rocks to come back to our spot. She stands over me, and I manage to dodge a stream of cold water as she wrings her hair out. In the water, it's less of a sunny strawberry blonde, and more burnished gold.

I need to stop fucking thinking about her like this.

"Big baby," Roisin laughs at me.

I roll my eyes. "Roisin..."

"I told you. Call me Ro."

I shake my head. "That's a nickname."

"And?"

"People who are close have nicknames. Family. Friends."

Roisin looks at me, and I regret my words immediately because some of the joy has faded. "And we're not friends, are we, American?"

I hate how she calls me that.

And I never want it to change.

"No," I say firmly. "We're not friends."

I don't know how to describe what we are. On paper, she's the agent in charge of keeping me hidden until I need to testify.

But we live together.

We act like a couple. Our cover is that we're a couple.

All of the work with none of the benefits, and what's killing me is that every day I spend with her, the act of being her partner feels less and less like work.

And more like life.

Not to mention, the benefits?

I fucking want them.

With every day that passes, I'm more acutely aware of how sexually attracted I am to this Interpol agent. I can never act on it, of course.

But fuck if I don't *dream.*

Roisin settles on the blanket next to me with a sigh. She puts her head on my shoulder, sending my confusion through the roof.

When we're in town, it makes sense for us to touch. We have to look like a happy couple, to keep up the charade.

But here?

She doesn't need to do it here. There's no one around.

Except me.

So what is real, and what isn't?

I don't fucking know.

But instead of spending all of my time worrying about it, I wrap an arm around her. The salt on her skin is rapidly drying, sticking to my fingers.

I want to lick it off.

"You know, I was convinced when I was a child that I'd see a selkie here," she murmurs.

"Selkie?" I ask.

Roisin nods. "It's a woman who can wear the skin of a seal. She swims in the ocean as a seal and comes on land at night to try and seduce men."

"Like a mermaid," I say.

She nods. "Very. Except she literally takes off her skin and hides it. It was said that the man who found her skin would control her, and I always thought that was sad."

"Why?" I ask, genuinely curious.

Roisin shrugs. "Because it taught me that if someone knows your secrets, they own you," she murmurs.

Not for the first time, I wonder what secrets Roisin is hiding.

I look down, noticing something for the first time. "What's this scar from?" I ask, my fingers gently tracing it.

She shivers, and the sight of her skin under my fingertips makes me rock hard again.

"My brother," she whispers.

She's talked about her brother before. He sounds like he was a real asshole, and it always makes me wonder if Caterina says the same thing about me.

"You want to share more?"

She looks back, her eyes sparkling. "And let you steal my secrets, American? I think not."

Then, with a laugh, she's up again, sprinting into the sea.

And the salt on my fingertips is all I have to remind me of the woman that I'd been holding.

I sigh.

That was one of the good memories. before I found out who she really was.

The woman under the skin.

I take a deep breath.

I have to show up for this fucking trial in three weeks. And part of the reason I don't want to isn't just because I'm not quite sure how to navigate what's going to happen.

It's because I have to see her again.

Roisin.

Who I thought was Roisin Kennedy.

But is really Roisin MacAntyre. Sister to the man Elio killed.

And only daughter of the Irish MacAntyre family.

2

ROISIN

I've been dreading the New Year because it means that I'm one day closer to seeing him again.

And I really, really don't want to see Marco De Luca.

Now.

Or ever.

Not after how we ended things, anyway. Because if I were to see him again?

I think that he might end up killing me.

The fact that Marco knows my secret is a continual thorn in my side. I wake up, wondering if today's the day that he'll use that information to his gain.

If today's the day that it will all blow up on me.

It's exhausting.

"Got your head in the clouds again, Roisin?"

I roll my eyes, taking the coffee that my boss, Seamus O'Hara, offers me. We stepped out of the office around midday, initially for lunch, but we decided to get coffee instead. Neither one of us is particularly interested in getting back into the flow of the Interpol station today. Seamus spent the holiday with his family, and I...

I spent it alone.

I shake my head. "You know I've never got my head anywhere but firmly on my shoulders," I snort.

Seamus winks at me. "Ah, but you're allowed to dream. You do know that, don't you?"

No. I want to scream at him. *I'm not allowed to dream. I'm not allowed to do anything, except scurry from one moment in my life to the next, like some kind of goddamn rat.*

The secrets are my problem. I used to think that it was cool to have so many secrets. I surrounded myself in them, wrapped like a blanket in a hundred of them.

I never thought that they could come unraveled.

At least, not like this.

"Seriously Ro, what's gotten into you today?" Seamus looks over, worry in his eyes. "You've always been so... together. And today you're just... not."

I huff and take a sip of the coffee. The streets of Dublin still bear some of the trappings of the post-holiday celebrations. The gutters smell like piss and vomit, but the trees contain merry pieces of tinsel or glitter, twinkling sadly in the wet Irish air.

"Nothing,' I lie, feeling the secret burn my tongue with bitterness. "Just thinking about the trial."

"Ah, that. No worries, darlin'," Seamus beams. "With your star witness, the trial is going to be an absolute breeze."

It takes everything in me to keep from wincing.

My star witness.

Meaning, the man that I was supposed to keep in custody. The one that Seamus, and every other Interpol agent in Ireland, thinks I still have in my custody.

The one I let walk away from me after he found out my last name. My brothers.

My rotten, foul legacy.

"Yes," I say through teeth that are clenched so tight, it's a miracle my teeth haven't cracked. "He's ready to go."

The fact that I have no idea where in the world Marco De Luca is sits on my chest like a damn weighted blanket.

You let him go, Ro. You're the one who didn't stop him once he saw the tattoo.

The circumstances around how, and why, Marco De Luca saw my MacAntyre tattoo are...

Well.

I certainly can't think about them for very long.

Not in public, anyway.

It takes a physical effort for me to shake off the memory of that day. Of his hands on my skin. Of the moment he found it, the falter in his voice...

Who are you really, Roisin?

My mentor's voice breaks me out of my thoughts. "Well, I'm off to do the paperwork for the day. The world may have taken a holiday, but crime did not," Seamus winks at me. I wave him away, then turn on my heel.

Guilt floods me.

Seamus is a good boss. He's been kind to me, and helped me grow through the years. The fact that I lie to him all day, every day....

It used to be fine.

Now, however, I feel much less 'fine' about it.

I huff, sipping the coffee and considering my options.

I could go into the office. I'm certain that my own stack of paperwork is excessive, but...

Unfortunately, I have bigger fish to fry.

Such as finding out where the hell Marco De Luca is.

And whether or not he's going to stand up at trial and testify, as he's told me he would.

Because if I don't find him, I'm going to be looking at not only losing my job, but a number of charges long enough to put me in jail too.

Right alongside the criminals that I have put there.

Instead of going into the office, I take my coffee and get into my car and head back to the little cottage in the village outside of the city. It's my official residence, for now anyway.

Well.

It's supposed to be, as I was supposed to utilize it in order to keep my charge from danger.

My hand drifts to the front gate, my fingers lingering. I push it open, my ears mindful, as ever, of the complete lack of squeak.

Marco fixed that.

He actually did a great deal of work on the little cottage, fixing things here and there as he stayed over the course of a few months. His touch is everywhere in the cottage, and I can't hardly look more than a foot without seeing something that reminds me of him.

Which, of course, means that every foot of the cottage punches me in the gut with the anxiety over Marco De Luca, over and over again.

Huffing, I finish off my coffee and toss it in the bin, settling into my couch as I open my laptop. For weeks, I've been searching for evidence of Marco. I'm not entirely sure why, because it's not like I can tell the other agents that I lost him.

They can't help me take him back in. I can't admit what I've done.

Because if I tug at even one lie, the whole damn thing is going to come unraveled.

If I told the other agents about Marco, then I'd have to tell them that he left because I'm a MacAntyre. And if they know I'm a MacAntyre, they're going to get very rightfully suspicious about why I'm working for Interpol.

And they're going to start to question some of the decisions I've made. The arrests. The convictions for crimes that eerily follow the lines of influence...especially the ones that benefit the family.

It's yet another lie, layered in with all the others. One that I've held close to my chest for years.

One that I hate myself for keeping, if I'm honest.

Because it's one of the only ones I'm ashamed of.

I'm just about to dig into some surveillance footage when the creak of my wood floor catches me by surprise.

I freeze.

There are no other sounds, save for the birds outside and the occasional rumble of a vehicle down the street.

Quietly, I place my laptop on the coffee table. I creep over to where my gun is, resting in its official holster, and slip the leather over my shoulders.

The creakiest floor in the cottage is near the back door. Pistol raised, I creep through the house, making no sound...

The floor squeaks again.

In a fluid motion, I click the safety off of the gun and step into the doorway. "Hands where I can fuckin' see them,' I snarl, pointing the gun in front of me at the shape in my kitchen.

"I guess that's one way to greet your brother," a voice says in response.

I keep my gun trained on him.

In front of me, a man turns. Green eyes, our father's eyes, in a face that is ripped straight from my nightmares, looks back at me.

"Hello, Sis," my brother Liam says with a smile.

I sigh.

There's no joy or love lost between us, so instead of returning his smile, I point the gun at him.

"The fuck are you doing in my house?"

Liam shrugs. 'Haven't heard from you in a while. Thought I'd drop by."

I roll my eyes, clicking the safety back onto the gun. I put it back in my shoulder holster, but don't put it away.

Liam raises his eyebrows. "You feeling saucy today, luchóg?"

The ugly nickname makes me bristle. "I'm not a mouse anymore, brother."

"Aye well. That you're not," he gestures to the gun.

Good.

"How can I help you?"

Liam sighs and flops into a chair. He looks over at me, his eyes...

Tired.

Liam has always been the more sane of my brothers. Unfortunately, he was raised separately from Kieran and I.

I didn't know that Kieran had a twin for the longest time. When I first saw Liam, all that I could think was how afraid I was that there were two of them.

I still don't think that I trust Liam. Not fully. It's hard to, since almost every scar on my body was put there by the man who looked just like him.

Liam's eyes, green just like mine, lack the fire and craziness of Kieran's.

And, I note for the first time that he looks tired as well.

"Congratulate me, sister. I'm getting married."

I cough. "What?"

"Married. In a month or two, I'll bring home a new bride."

"I didn't know you were dating," I say softly.

Liam doesn't smile. "I'm not."

"Okay..."

"It's more of... an arrangement. A strategic alliance to ensure that there's peace among a couple of key allies."

"Like who?" I can't help but ask.

Liam shrugs. "Do you have any new information for me?"

I turn, bile rising in my throat. "Interpol is following the Garda lead on some of the recent kidnappings in Cork. They think that someone is trying to antagonize shipping lanes."

Liam swears softly in Gaelic, then stands. "I think we'll need to move the date of the wedding."

"To when? And who's the poor girl? Is she... does she know why you're doing this?"

He nods. "She volunteered."

A small part of me sighs in relief. I'm not sure why, but envisioning yet another woman caught in this whole web of lies feels...

Bad.

Worse, somehow, than the place I've spun for myself.

"Who is she?"

"Anastasia Novikov."

I blink. "The model?"

"Aye."

I look over at him. "Liam, isn't she..."

"She's also a physicist," he says, looking down at his black leather boots.

Interesting.

The tone in his voice is almost defensive.

"She's wildly famous," I say.

He nods.

"Isn't she a little... high profile for you?"

"That's the point, sister."

"Oh," I murmur.

I have to hand it to him. It's actually a smart move. Because if he's married to a very rich, very famous Russian, it will be harder for him to be targeted by the numerous enemies that Kieran racked up over the course of his tenure as the leader of our family.

Liam glances at me. "Marco is going to testify against us, isn't he?"

I sigh. "Liam, you know..."

He holds up a hand. "I do. I know. But we can't have the attention. Not now," he says gently.

I nod.

Kieran ruined the family business. He involved us in dark, horrible things, holding us all prisoner.

Forcing me, a young Interpol agent, to be a double agent. I would give him information...

And he wouldn't kill my mother.

Kieran and Liam and I share a father. My mother, a short-term relationship that happened outside of my father's marriage, has been hidden.

From me.

For the majority of my life.

Kieran, however, knew where she was. That information died with him.

Liam and I have been working together to find her. I've always been convinced that, working for Interpol, she'll show up.

Eventually.

Kieran twisted that desire to his will. Liam asks me to keep it going, for the survival of our family.

I shouldn't do it but...

I do.

"Just keep him from saying anything to harm us."

"It would be helpful if our brother hadn't tried to brutally murder his sister," I snap.

Murder, of course, being the kindest fate that Caterina Rossi could have met that night.

"Aye," Liam nods. "But now we're allied with the Rossi's."

"How?"

He grins. "Wedding bells."

My eyes open. "Anastasia."

"Yes. So. I need to get married. Before the trial. And Marco needs to keep his mouth shut."

"He will, if that's the case."

Liam shakes his head. "We don't know what he'll say. Marco De Luca may be allied with Elio, but he's always been his own person. Clearly," he says, eyebrow raised. "As I don't think he's here right now, is he?"

I don't answer that question.

With a sigh, Liam stands. "I won't bother you further, sister. But be careful of Marco De Luca. He's dangerous. Can't be trusted. Will he be back in time?"

"Yes," I say confidently.

Liam looks at me, his eyebrow raised.

"He will," I insist.

Shaking his head, Liam heads for the door. "He better be. Or all of this is going to come down. And we're going to be to blame."

3

ROISIN

The date of the trial inches closer, and every day that I can't find Marco feels like another day that I'm drowning.

Finally, it's the night before. I'm sitting on my couch, listening to the same punk rock record that I've been listening to since I was a mere eight years old.

I can't explain it, but the clashing of the music makes me feel... settled, somehow.

Complete, in a way that I've never been able to before.

Eyes shut, I picture how the trial is going to go tomorrow. It's just the beginning, a hearing to get everything going. But if Marco doesn't show, it's going to be clear that I lost him.

That he hasn't been in my custody.

Which is going to get me fired. So fired, in fact, that I may have an investigation directed at me. Which would lead to the inevitable outcome of Seamus, and my entire team, finding out that I'm the bastard MacAntyre child.

Which would definitely lead to not only my arrest, but the arrest of my brother, and...

"Your taste in music really needs to evolve."

I shoot up off the couch.

Standing in front of me, darkening the doorway to my fucking kitchen, is Marco De Luca.

For a second I'm just struck by the presence that he has.

Marco isn't just a person. I swear to God he's like a force of nature. Standing in the doorway, backlit from my crap kitchen light, his dark gaze sears into me, like some kind of primal god of storms.

His hair is dark, but flecked in places with silver. I know he's not old, exactly, but pushing toward forty, a solid decade older than I am. I like that he hasn't done anything about the flecks of lightness there.

I like that he doesn't seem to care.

I know, however, that the choice is probably intentional. Because everything about Marco is intentional. Even the outfit he has on, jet black pants and an equally black button-down shirt, must have been chosen because of its complete lack of remarkable.

Or, the ability that it gives him to blend into the shadows.

His face looks like it's carved from marble. Tan skin, dark eyes beneath eyebrows that are more than a little severe, and a Roman nose all give him a very, very stern face.

However, his lips ruin the harshness of his other features. They're unfairly plump, and they remind me of every sinful fantasy that I've ever had about him.

Some of those fantasies, though, aren't just fantasies...

They're memories.

I remember his lips, and how they curved over mine. How they demanded, with words and actions, that I open for him.

How they look wrapped around my nipple. How they feel, skating over my skin.

The tender touch of them before they hit the edge of the tattoo...

Fuck.

"Marco," I say, finally standing to do something about the record that's screeching at us still. I pull the needle off of the record, the slight scratch a jarring noise that sets my nerves on edge.

I tell myself that, anyway. And that it's not the presence of Marco, crackling over my shoulder like a thundercloud.

"I see you made it back just fine," I mutter.

I'm not sure why I'm trying to provoke him. He's still just... standing there. Taking up space in the doorway to my kitchen.

Staring.

For a second, my mind goes straight to the fact that Marco De Luca isn't exactly my friend.

After all, my brother kidnapped his sister. Tried to kidnap his niece. Killed one of his aunts.

His track record with the MacAntyre clan isn't really stellar.

Something in me, though, doesn't think that he's here to hurt me.

He came back. The night before the trial.

If he didn't want to show up for it...

He wouldn't have.

"Marco. Say something," I bark.

He shifts, moving forward. For a second I think he's going to touch me, but then he brushes past me...to the stairs.

"Marco," I whisper. I'm not sure if he can hear me.

I'm not sure I want him to.

The stairs creak under his weight. I listen to the familiar pattern of him going up to the little loft room, then hear him pause before the last step.

"I was always going to come back."

His voice is a low rumble. It's cultured in a way that I never expect. Marco is, after all, a gangster.

He shouldn't talk like he's a fucking prince.

The stairs resume their squeaking, and I listen to him move around upstairs. I haven't taken out any of his clothing or anything, since I wasn't sure what to do with it.

Or were you hopeful that he would come back?

I slam the thought away, mentally trying to make sure that I don't entertain anything so foolish as that thought.

Marco didn't come back to resume the little charade we'd been living.

He came back for business. To keep his word.

He comes down the stairs again, and heads to the couch.

Quietly, he pulls the couch bed out and begins to put sheets on it.

I watch him.

Finally, Marco turns to look at me. The silence between us is so thick, I can feel it pressing down on my ears, clogging my ability to hear anything.

Finally, he licks his lips, and I'm embarrassed at how quickly the gesture makes me blush.

"You should go to bed. The hearing will be early," he grunts.

Then, clearly dismissing me, he turns.

I can take a fucking hint, and I have enough pride to keep myself from saying anything else.

I turn on my heel marching up the stairs. I may have a million questions right now, but I know one thing for sure.

Marco De Luca may have come back.

But he sure as hell didn't come back for me.

The journey to Dublin for the hearing is so awkward. In order to preserve his status in witness protection, Marco will arrive at the hearing separately, but it's my job to complete the hour drive and drop him off with Seamus at the meeting point. Then, I'll park, go to the office and get into my official Interpol-sanctioned court attire, and meet them there. Marco's identity will be preserved, and he'll give anonymous testimony about the incident in Belarus, as well as the new developments of the explosion at a café in Amsterdam, to a panel of solicitors and judges.

We don't speak on the way there.

And, the sound of the silence is absolutely killing me.

Marco is invading all of my other senses. I swear that I can feel the electricity of his presence on my skin. I can smell him, and it just puts me back to our last night together. The sight of him out of the corner of my eye makes me want to just turn and stare, narrow Irish roads be damned.

Finally, about five minutes before the drop off, I can't take it anymore.

"Marco. Talk to me."

He shifts, wincing like my words have some kind of physical impact on him. The silence stretches, endless and twisting.

Finally, he huffs. "I have nothing to say to you, Roisin."

I've always been annoyed by the fact that he won't use my nickname.

But now, I just miss the way he used to say my name. Like a benediction.

Now, he says it like a curse.

"Marco, you-"

"We're here," he interrupts.

That we are.

I put the car in park, looking down as Marco unbuckles his seat.

He doesn't look back.

The door opens, my shit car groaning as Marco shifts. I blink, my eyes unexpectedly hot as I look out after him.

I wait for him to say something. Anything.

The door slams instead.

Blinking back tears that I didn't know were there, I put the car in drive and head to the office.

By the time I get there, I've mostly composed myself. My heart rate is somewhat normal, and I don't feel the need to explode into a basket case of tears anymore.

At least, I don't think so.

I park in my assigned spot, then take the back staircase to the main entrance. Once there, I scan my badge, pressing against the gate as I wait for it to open...

The electronic beep of denial greets me instead.

I frown, scanning my badge again. The light, which always lights up green to allow me access, flashes.

Red.

I blink.

"Ms. Kennedy?"

Colin, the security agent who supervises the door, is coming over. I shoot him a smile and wave my badge at him.

"Hey Col. For some reason my badge doesn't seem to work..."

My voice trails off as I see the look in his eyes.

"I need you to come with me," he says, his voice solemn.

It's the seriousness that makes me flinch.

Silently, my heart in my throat, I follow Colin.

Straight into one of the interrogation rooms.

. . .

I've been sitting at the table, sweating, for what feels like an hour before I finally hear the door click open.

I look up, my palms sweating, as Seamus enters the room.

"Seamus," I breathe. "What the hell is going on?"

His face is drawn, making my heart sink.

"When were you going to tell us that you were related to Kieran MacAntyre?"

Fuck.

I pale. "Seamus, I..."

"Stop. Just stop," he says, holding up a hand. "I'm going to need you to start from the beginning, Ro. Tell me everything."

I hesitate.

The part of me that's a trained law enforcement official wants to trust him. I want to tell him everything, just like he's asking me to do.

But the other part of me, who grew up among hardened criminals, is a little more concerned. I wouldn't say that alarms are going off with Seamus, exactly, but something is sketchy about this situation.

I take a deep breath, and settle for everything except the fact that I'm selling information to my brother.

"My mother was William MacAntyre's mistress," I say. "I'm younger than my twin brothers, and she managed to keep me hidden from him until I was ten years old. When I was ten, William found out about me and... decided that I would live with him and Kieran," I say.

Seamus is staring at me.

Gulping, I continue. "She disappeared, Seamus. Gone. I knew she wasn't dead because my father would get drunk and... he would get drunk and wonder where she was."

Seamus gives me a look, but I'm not going to give him more than that. Detailing how my father used to beat the hell out of me, blaming me for having my mother's face, isn't something I want to go into right now.

Instead, I hold my head up high. "I ran away as soon as I passed my graduation. Took the exam for the academy the next day. By the time Kieran and William knew I was gone, I was safely at Interpol."

What I don't tell him is how, years later, Kieran broke into my apartment in Dublin. How he showed me exactly how cruel he could be, and then showed me the picture of my mother.

My mother, who I joined Interpol to find.

My mother, who Kieran somehow knew was alive. Knew her location.

And I didn't.

He told me he'd kill her.

Unless I started reporting to him, as well as my boss.

Seamus sighs and slaps a file down. "For your honesty, Ro," he says softly.

Greedily, I grab the file and rip it open.

Reading it, my jaw drops. I look up at Seamus.

"I didn't do this."

He nods. "I know."

I shut the file. "Seamus. I swear. I didn't orchestrate that attack..."

"I know, Ro."

I shut my mouth and push the file back.

Seamus sighs. "At about six o'clock this morning, this email came across our desk. It was mine and one other higher up, and I knew the second that I saw it, it was bullshit. I figured that you might be related to Kieran, but I didn't know how."

I nod.

"For you to have put together that attack, you would have had to have been in two places at once. Because we also have a record of you here. Photo evidence here."

I tap the file. "But there's someone who looks like me here too..."

"I know, Ro. You're being framed."

The word rocks me. "Framed?"

Seamus nods, and I sit back in my seat.

"But how..."

"My guess is an enemy of your brother."

My eyes widen. "How do they know I'm related to him?"

"That, I think, is something we need to find out. Who else knows that you're a MacAntyre?"

If I could take away my ability to emote, right then and there, I would.

Because the second Seamus sees my face, he sighs. He leans down and picks up the radio.

"Bring De Luca in."

4

MARCO

THIS ISN'T HOW IT'S SUPPOSED TO GO.

It's been a fucking whirlwind of a forty-eight hour time. I've gone from the cold, early January landscape of upstate New York to the dreary gray of an Irish January, and I still have no fucking plan about how I'm going to testify in this hearing.

I don't know how to protect everyone. My family. My legacy.

Roisin.

The whole flight, my heart practically burned every time I thought of her name. I went back and forth on what to do. Part of me wanted to walk into this hearing and immediately tell all of them that she's a liar. That she's a MacAntyre, one of the most hardened crime families in Ireland.

Then, I would feel guilty. Awful.

Like a fucking piece of shit.

Because exposing Roisin as a MacAntyre would clearly screw over whatever life she's trying to build for herself.

She never told me why or how, but I also know that she doesn't exactly have a great relationship with her brothers.

Well.

The dead one, anyway.

I know that Liam didn't live with her and Kieran during his childhood. She was raised with Kieran, if the rumors that I've heard are accurate.

And Kieran was one nasty motherfucker.

I don't know why I expected Roisin to be... different.

Well. She did choose a life with Interpol over a life with her brother, so I guess I did expect something different from her.

I wrestled with all of it through the flight. Through the ride to the cottage. Through touching the gate that I fixed for her. Through everything, I couldn't figure out what the fuck I was going to do...

But I was still drawn to her.

After feeling the emptiness at my family's holiday, Roisin called to me like a lighthouse.

Even if I hated her as much as I was compelled to follow the light that led to her.

When I saw her on the couch, listening to that god-awful music that she's obsessed with, I had to stop.

I consider myself a relatively articulate man. I have to be. I've always had to be.

But the sight of Roisin on the couch, her hair catching the light, her peaches-and-cream skin flushed as she hummed along to the brutal racket?

I didn't have words for that moment.

Well.

I didn't have the right words for the moment.

I wanted to tell her that I've fucking missed her. That she's the most beautiful fucking thing I've ever seen. That every day since I walked out on her, I've fantasized about touching her and her soft as fuck skin again.

That I'ved tried to see other women, to be around them. To get her out of my mind.

But I fucking can't.

And then, of course, it crashes down on me that she's not just my Roisin.

She's the sister of my sworn fucking enemy. Liam MacAntyre, the man that I have a hesitating, temporary alliance with.

The man whose brother killed my parents.

It couldn't be anyone but the MacAntyres. It simply couldn't.

They're the fucking worst.

I don't want to remember, either, that she's been lying to me. That she withheld her true identity from me.

And that she might have been spying on me, selling that information to either one of her brothers... the whole fucking time.

And then, I definitely couldn't say shit. Because the warring emotions inside of me, if they came out, would have made me seem utterly and totally insane.

So instead, I ignored her. Stomped past her to set up the little couch sleeper, and I didn't sleep at all.

I thought about her. Every creak from the loft bedroom upstairs, I thought of her. Every single noise made me think…

of her.

Now, I'm waiting to be picked up by whatever Interpol handler comes next.

And I still have no fucking clue how to handle this hearing.

"Marco," a male voice calls.

I turn.

Only to be met with a fist to the face.

I don't think.

I react.

My body goes into a brutal, efficient, fighting mode.

Most people in my line of work have to be relatively competent at defending themselves. It's just part of the work.

I, however, never settle for being competent.

Which means that when it comes to hand-to-hand combat?

I am fucking exceptional.

Within seconds I have my attacker in a headlock, and he's writhing underneath me. I flex my bicep that's pulled around his neck, and he gasps, panting, as he tries to breathe.

"Who the fuck are you?" I snarl.

Clearly, he's not Interpol.

The man curses in Russian, and I tighten. "Who. The fuck. Sent you," I growl.

"Stop! Police!"

Fucking hell.

I don't want this asshole to get away. I bear down, hoping he'll pass out, when I hear a familiar whine behind me.

My brain has two seconds to form one word... Taser.

Then, the electricity hits me, and everything goes still.

Trussed like a fucking pig, I glower at the set of agents who took me in.

I'm sitting in one of the Interpol interrogation rooms, my hands bound in front of me at the wrists. I'm glaring up at the agents, who are doing their best to whisper in the corner.

Fucking cops.

A radio crackles slightly, and one of them lifts it. I hear my name, and they both look at me.

I dare them to fucking touch me. I fucking dare...

"Up, De Luca," one of them sneers. "You're fucking lucky you haven't been booked yet."

I resist the urge to tell them that Interpol isn't concerned with petty assault, but I let them hustle me into another interrogation room.

Once inside, I fix my face, my features assuming a mask...

Then, I see who else is there.

"Roisin," I breathe.

I can't help it.

She's sitting at the interrogation table, in the position of someone being interrogated. Her eyes are red-rimmed, like she's about to cry, and her pale skin is nearly bloodless.

My first instinct is concern.

My next?

Rage.

"What the fuck did they do to you?" I snarl.

Roisin pales further. "Marco..."

"Sit, De Luca," another voice barks.

I hadn't noticed, but an older Irish man is seated across from her. The minions who hauled me in here provide a chair, and I glower at them until they back off.

Like a king ascending his throne, I sit.

The older man nods to the other two. "You can leave."

"Agent O'Hara, we caught him assaulting someone in public..."

"You can leave," he repeats.

Without any protest, they walk away.

He turns to me. "Mister De Luca, would there be any reason you assaulted a man in broad daylight?"

I tilt my head. "He started it?"

"Interesting," O'Hara nods. "Did he really?"

"Would you believe me either way?"

"Surprisingly, Mr. De Luca, I think you'll find that honesty is the best currency with me."

The level look in his eyes is... warm.

But, the steel behind it is there as well.

I decide to tell a version of the truth that isn't necessarily a lie. "A Russian called my name, came in swinging. I swung back."

"How did you know he was Russian?"

I arch an eyebrow. "I've had enough Russians cuss me out to recognize what he was saying."

O'Hara chuckles at that. "Well, there's some truth to that, then." He turns to Roisin. "I don't know if a Russian would be an enemy of your family?"

My heart skips.

Did he know?

Did everyone fucking know but me?

If that's the case, why the fuck am I the last to know?

Roisin shrugs. "My brother is marrying one, so..."

"How do you know about Novikov?" I interrupt.

It's Roisin's turn to raise an eyebrow now. "You think that I don't know about my own brother's wedding?"

I huff.

"Roisin is... the center of a place she doesn't need to be central to. It isn't her fault that her family is who they are, but all the same, she's being blamed for some incidents."

"Incidents?" I ask.

O'Hara gives me a raised eyebrow. "Indeed. A certain explosion, most recently in Amsterdam, that I believe a certain Salvatore De Luca and a Gia Rossi were also implicated in."

"They were absolved of that," I say quickly.

O'Hara's eyebrows pinch together. 'Indeed they were. Because of overwhelming evidence that a certain Irish family had done it instead."

Oh.

Fuck.

"Roisin wasn't there. She had me in custody at that time, and we were awaiting trial," I respond in a stiff voice.

I don't want to think about that time. It was before I knew about Roisin.

Before I knew her family name, but also before I knew what she tasted like, and the little moan she makes when she...

Shut. The fuck. Up.

I manage to snarl at myself convincingly enough, and the urge to think about Roisin that night fades.

Barely.

"I am aware of Ms. Kennedy's whereabouts that day," O'Hara says. "As her supervisor, I was aware of all of her assignments as your cover for the witness protection program."

She ducks, her eyes looking down at the table, and a strange, smug satisfaction creeps over me.

Not aware of all of the activities, are you then?

"Still, the leak to the press that calls Roisin's integrity into question is... interesting. There is no mention that she is an Interpol agent, which means that most likely, whoever is trying to frame her is doing so from..."

"My world," I breathe.

O'Hara nods.

I frown. "I don't think anyone from my family knows about.. who she is."

Roisin's face tightens. "The only people who know are Irish."

"Then I believe you will need to start there," O'Hara says.

We both blink.

"Start there?" Roisin repeats.

He nods. "Someone needs to figure out why this information was leaked. And who better to do it than you?"

"She can't do it on her own," I blurt.

Roisin's eyes narrow, and she glares at me like a queen surveying scum on the face of the earth.

It's the challenge in her eyes that I like so fucking much.

"I don't need help," she mutters.

O'Hara snorts. "And what if the person who started the rumor decides to kill you, hmm? It's better to have some kind of way for you to access help if you need it."

"I can find out who is doing this to me."

O'Hara shakes his head. "Not if there's someone trying to frame you. Right now, you're wanted by Interpol."

Her jaw drops. "But..."

"I've gone out on a limb for you, lass," he says softly.

Roisin's face tightens. I'm expecting gratitude, or even appreciation. However, her expression looks more like...

Guilt.

"Here's the task. You have thirty days. That's as long as I can buy you. Thirty days to find out who is trying to frame you, and then I have to take you in."

Roisin nods. "Understood."

I shuffle. I'm still not quite sure why I'm here, other than the obvious.

The connection to my brother Sal, and my sister-in-law, Gia, stands pretty clear.

But, it's not like I can do anything to actually help her. And on top of that, I'm not even certain that I want to.

Despite the fact that it's fucking killing you to not be able to do anything?

I want to growl with frustration. Roisin lied to me. Her past identity is getting her in trouble.

What the fuck does it matter to me if she's having a hard time.

O'Hara turns to me, seemingly sensing my distress. "And you're to give testimony soon, right?"

"Yes," I mutter hesitantly.

"Well then. I think that you're first on the list of people who stand to gain from framing our Roisin for this," he says.

I narrow my eyes. What the fuck is he..

"And if you did that, it would be a very long time in jail for you, and for that brother of yours, wouldn't it?"

"Sal didn't set off that explosion. Or the one in Belarus," I snarl.

O'Hara's eyebrows pinch. "Did I say anything about the explosion in Belarus?"

Fuck.

"Well. I believe that in that situation, a certain Russian mob princess was captured. And, if this is to be believed, said princess is now about to be wed to one Liam MacAntyre?"

Shit.

The threads of what he's spinning are finally coming together. I tilt my head. "You want me to help her."

"Aye."

"Why?" I can't help but ask.

O'Hara studies me. "Marco De Luca. Heir to a family name that died out in the 80s. Heir to a shipping company that's been all but absorbed. Brother to a family that has essentially moved on. Even with the recent development of your Dino becoming the head of a certain cartel from Brazil, it seems that I no longer have anything to fear from you... and I have no use for you," he says quietly.

It's like a fucking slap in the face.

I bristle, and O'Hara chuckles. "Aye, bluster all you want, but it's the truth. You've somehow worked yourself out of a job, setting up cozy lives for all your siblings. And don't mistake me, I've seen the chess games you've played with your siblings. They're well done," he winks. "However, you've created a place for everyone except yourself. You can choose to help our Roisin. Or, you can walk away."

His words... hurt.

Each one is like a fucking cut.

But strangely, it's like being punched in the face by a friend.

He's not wrong.

It's why I feel so empty. He's absolutely right. I've essentially created a place for myself where I don't exist inside the life that my family does. I have worked myself out of a job. Out of a life. I've done things to set everyone else up... except myself.

I did it, and I literally made them into a perfect fucking picture.

Without me.

Elio's offer to bring me 'back into the fold' burned at my heart, and I didn't at the time know why.

But now, I do.

And somehow, this ancient Irish cop was the only one to see it.

I don't know what to do with this information, and the anger that's clutching at my throat threatens to choke me.

O'Hara, to his credit, seems to smirk. I know that he knows he's got me right where he wants me.

But fuck.

He's not fucking wrong.

I'm seething, and Roisin's eyes narrow. I can see her pick herself up and puff her chest, like she's going to defend me.

Her pretty mouth opens. "Marco is a valuable asset-"

"Marco is nothing now. Marco De Luca is as valuable as a newborn kitten to our work. He's irrelevant, now," O'Hara snaps.

This fucking... "I'll do it."

Roisin's eyes snap to mine, and I meet her green gaze.

"I'll fucking do it," I repeat.

O'Hara makes a sound, but I'm not listening.

I'm watching her.

And wondering if this is a big fucking mistake.

5

ROISIN

Seamus grins like a cat that's caught the canary. "There's a good lad."

Marco, who decidedly does *not* look like a good lad, or like he wants to be challenged by anyone in the slightest, glares at my mentor.

I'm still not certain what happened.

The walls of the interrogation room seem smaller than ever. It feels somehow hot and cold in here at the same time, and I can't seem to get past the fact that I'm being *framed*.

For something that I most definitely didn't do.

In fact, I didn't even come close to doing this.

Not only was I not in Amsterdam around that time, but I was literally under security surveillance. I had to check in with Seamus every other day, and there's simply no way I would have been able to plant anything.

However.

I'm certain that wouldn't matter.

The thing about being framed is that whoever is doing the framing usually knows exactly what they're doing.

In this case, I see the trap. If I were to come out and say that I didn't set up the bomb because I was an Interpol agent who is in charge of protective custody for a sensitive witness, it would mean several things.

First, Interpol would have to admit that they're still chasing the De Luca family, tipping off anyone who is connected with the De Lucas. While they may not be a large family, their connection to the Rossi family, and now my own, is something noteworthy.

To a lot of people.

Interpol isn't loyal to me, or any of the agents that it has. If we pose a risk, we're going to get cut to maintain the safety and security of the organization.

Point.

Blank.

There's no way around it, and we're all trained on the protocols when we sign up. I know it's not a mystery to me.

I just never thought I would have to deal with…

this .

Whoever is framing me knows. They know that if I sit and do nothing, it will look like I planted the bomb in Amsterdam that nearly killed Sal and Gia De Luca, and did kill two high-ranking Russian officials. Because the Russians were there, they'll link it to the bombing in Belarus, when Kieran kidnapped Anastasia Novikov and she appeared a week later, unharmed, at the Cannes film festival.

I saw the ghosts of bruises on her perfect-looking skin.

But I also knew where to look.

The idea that Anastasia Novikov could be my sister in law....

"Ro?"

I jump.

Seamus is studying me, and I give him a weak smile. "Sorry. Head in the clouds, I guess."

He rolls his eyes, and Marco gives me a strange look.

You've never once had your head in the clouds, his eyes seem to say.

Oddly, I find that to be a compliment that makes me... kind of proud.

"Well. Let's get it out of the clouds and back in the room, hmm?"

I nod. "Okay. Thirty days to find out who is trying to frame me."

"Aye," Seamus nods. "I can't buy you more than thirty days, Ro."

I nod. "Okay. Liam told me that he's getting married to her soon, so I think that we can make that work."

"And what, exactly, is your plan?"

I turn.

There's only one way to play this.

"Looks like you and I are wedding dates, Marco."

He takes one look at me. His eyes flash, a chilling look that sends a shiver down my spine.

Then Marco turns to Seamus and holds up his handcuffed wrists.

"Lock me the fuck up."

Seamus does the exact opposite.

Within about an hour, we're both released. Seamus has passports ready, which seems suspicious considering that Marco has one as well.

Clearly, Seamus wasn't expecting either one of us to say no.

Passports in hand, a large amount of cash ready to go, Marco and I are dropped off by two junior agents, Flynn and Boyle, who seem to be more than a little pissed at Marco.

He glares right back at them.

I nod at the other agents. "Thanks, we've got it from here."

"I don't like this, Ro," Flynn says. He's giving Marco a nasty look and his hand is drifting to his taser. "I've seen the damage this fella can cause."

"Aye, nearly cracked the windpipe on that Russian bloke," Boyle adds.

I snort.

Because there's no way they've actually seen the type of damage that Marco can cause.

I, however, have.

"I'll be fine. Thank you, though," I murmur to them.

Boyle and Flynn give Marco one more nasty look before they leave.

And Marco and I are alone, at a bus depot in Dublin.

I take a deep breath. "We need to invent a backstory."

"Oh, that's what we need?" he barks.

I turn. "Look. Obviously someone is trying to frame me for all this. Odds are they come from somewhere in my brother's organization, because you're the only one who knows about me outside of that."

"And you think I wouldn't tell?" he sneers.

I blink. "No. I don't."

I didn't think Marco was going to go around blabbing my identity to everyone.

His eyebrows pinch.

I sigh again. "Look, Marco, I thought maybe you'd be angry enough to use it against me. I was thinking you'd show up at the hearing and tell all of Interpol who I was, just because you were mad that I'd... kept it from you," I murmur. "But you're not exactly the kind to spread rumors just because. You'd use them to your advantage, but you'd never just... be careless about it."

Marco's face goes through a series of motions, none of them particularly good. "Is that meant to be a compliment?"

"It's meant to be the truth," I snort.

His lips tighten. "Something you know little of."

"Oh shut up. Again, you're the master of using lies to your advantage," I snap at him.

Marco doesn't respond.

I shut my eyes, massaging the place between my eyebrows. "If we go to Liam, we have to tell him something..."

"We're together."

I blink. "What?"

"It's the only thing he'll believe," Marco says. "He knows that I've been gone, that I've been... engaging in the other affairs with my family. Elio and Liam have a new trade alliance, one they're cementing with his marriage to Stassi--"

"Stasi?"

He nods. "She prefers that. Anastasia is a mouthful."

The fact that Marco knows the nickname of a world-renowned model, and the way my stomach tightens around knowing it, is unsettling.

Mostly unsettling that I definitely, definitely seem to care.

"Okay. So how are we going to explain the fact that we're... together?" I say.

Marco gives me a look. "We're going to tell the truth."

"And what, exactly, is that?"

My voice is little more than a whisper.

I'm desperate to know his answer, both because I need to know it to convince Liam we're dating, and because...

I think I just need to know.

The urge to hear from him what we are, what we're doing, is almost burning at me.

Does he remember everything the same way I do?

Did it matter to him, like it mattered to me?

Marco looks at me. "You took me into custody, in the witness protection program. During that time we... connected," he says.

No. He doesn't say it.

He spits it out like he's ripping out a tooth.

"I needed to do some things to handle my family. I came back, and you told me you want to be with me and can't be an Interpol agent anymore."

I nod. "The agency is suppressing the framing. They quickly took the news article down and worked with the press," I add. Seamus let me know that right before we left.

Marco makes a hum, and my body prickles at the low, throaty noise.

"Now we're together and you want to introduce Liam and celebrate his wedding. You're coming back to the family," he says.

There's another note there, something bitter, as he says the word 'family'.

I want to ask so many things.

"Is it true?" I ask.

That's the question that I want to know the most.

Marco raises an eyebrow. "Surely you know we're not-"

"No," I interrupt. "That when we... when you and I were in the cottage. Did you develop feelings for me?"

Marco studies me for a minute longer.

"The best lies begin as truth, Roisin. Surely you know that, given your skill with the subject," he snaps.

I flinch.

"Marco..."

He holds up a hand. "Save it. I was a fool to think that you would have something real with me then. I'm a fucking criminal, and you're..." he studies me. "I don't know. You're either caught in something you can't get out of, or you're lying to everyone you've ever met. Either way, Roisin, I don't want anything to do with it. I'll help you with this, but after, we're done."

Ignoring the ache that his words bring, I take a deep breath. "Why help at all?"

Marco studies me.

"Your boss, Agent O'Hara, is right. I don't know how to set myself up for my own success. I only know how to do it for others. Might as well tie up this last loose end before I walk away entirely, leaving everyone else to the ends of their stories while I figure out what the fuck to do with mine."

Marco turns, marching toward the bus station, and I watch his back.

I'm not imagining it.

Seamus' words shook him to the core.

It sounds like both of us have had to deal with hard truths today.

And neither one of us is happy about it.

We end up taking a bus to a car dealership, where Marco walks in and out ten minutes later with the keys to a brand new Jaguar SUV.

I climb inside, looking at him. "Really?"

"What?" he says as the engine purrs to life.

"Isn't this car a little conspicuous?"

He rolls his eyes. "Would Liam expect me to show up in anything else, if I was truly in a relationship with his sister?"

Okay.

That's fair.

I make a little noise in my throat and look around at the car. It's gorgeous, of course. And Marco's right... no self-respecting mafia man would ever be caught dead in anything other than the most luxurious car in the world.

Especially if they were trying to impress one of their own.

The Jaguar growls as he revs the engine, and we turn onto one of Dublin's tiny streets. I'm expecting him to ask for directions or take the road out of town, but instead we pull up outside of a very expensive looking department store.

The valet comes for the door, and I look at Marco. "What are we doing here?"

He pulls out his wallet. "We're buying new clothes."

"But..."

"Again, do you want to make this work or not, Roisin?"

I blink.

Marco leans over. "You're going to buy yourself some clothes. They're going to be the most expensive, most luxurious versions of the clothes you would want. We're going to meet back here in three hours and you're going to tell me how to get to your brother's fucking house. Got it?"

I nod.

I can't help it. I'm not usually one who likes being told what to do, but the low, throaty command in Marco's voice is...

Electrifying.

The valet is practically knocking on the window now, and I let him open the door. Marco and I get out, and like a shadow, I follow him into the department store.

Inside, I'm immediately reminded that this isn't a regular store. When I was little, my mom shopped at all the bargain shops. When my dad found out about me, he tried to truss me up like his fucking mafia princess.

It didn't go well for him.

I'm an Interpol agent. I don't know anything about walking into a fancy department store.

Marco, however, does.

Within seconds he's greeted by someone who looks like she could have walked straight out of a magazine. Vogue Ireland then proceeds to hug Marco, which makes my blood absolutely boil until he turns around to look at me.

He winks.

Winks!

The bloody nerve of him!

He winks at me and then waves, and before I know it a flurry of people have descended on me.

What feels like an eternity later, I'm sitting in a dressing room. I've been prodded and poked and fluffed and stuffed into a million different outfits, and I am about to practice my fucking hand-to-hand skills.

This must be obvious, because eventually the attendants disappear.

I look at myself in the mirror.

"You look ridiculous," I mutter.

I'm wearing some kind of jumpsuit. It fits well... It's flattering enough. I'm by no means a tall, elegant, or even well-endowed woman. I've got wide hips and very athletic legs, and my breasts... exist.

But in this jumpsuit, they look downright plump.

Lovely.

I, however, am overstimulated and...

ugh.

Sad.

I've been fighting off memories of my father, dragging me to see a personal shopper when I was a teenager. He had a thousand critiques of my body then, when I needed them the absolute least.

When I needed my mom to fight them off.

But I didn't have it then.

Suddenly the jumpsuit is too tight. Too scratchy. It's not even helpful, really, because the fucking undergarments they pasted onto my body are also...

The door squeaks open.

Oh, I swear to god if this is that one with the undergarments...."Fuck off," I snap.

"I see that they haven't managed to dress the attitude yet."

I freeze.

A familiar shape steps into the dressing room, the door quietly closing behind him.

I refuse to turn.

So instead, I stare at him in the dressing room mirror.

On the contrary, his eyes are not on mine.

They're staring at the very, very expensive lingerie that's shaping my body.

I'm halfway out of the jumpsuit, so he hasn't seen the sorry excuse of lace that's covering me there, but he can certainly see what's on the top.

I'm kind of afraid to look away.

Also that would mean that I'm the one who looks away first.

"I don't like this shit, Marco," I say, deciding to break the tension.

I'm doing it on my terms.

And definitely not because his eyes are making me heat up like a furnace.

"You don't like what, Roisin?"

"Looking like... this," I say.

His eyes darken. They literally seem to turn an impossibly deeper shade of brown, until his irises are practically black.

He steps forward, and I resist the urge to shiver at the heat rolling off of him.

"You look good enough," he murmurs.

My nostrils flare in the mirror, and I can practically feel my heart beating in my chest.

"I look like a doll."

"If that's what you think," he murmurs.

The low rumble of his voice is enough to make my skin break out in goosebumps.

I don't want it to.

But unfortunately I have absolutely no control over that.

Marco leans down. He smells good. Expensive. He managed to change into a fully black outfit, which is somewhere between formal and murderous, and I can't really tell which direction it goes in.

Because I can't see it at all.

Because I'm trying so hard not to stare, but also to watch him, because his nose is dipping toward my neck...

"I think they look pretty fucking good," he growls.

He growls it.

Holy mother of god, I can't do this.

I go to take a step, but Marco's hands drift over my shoulders. He's not gripping me tightly or anything, I could easily walk away if I want, but...

The illusion is...

I shudder.

"Your skin is so soft, Roisin," Marco murmurs. His eyes catch mine in the mirror, and I lock our gazes. Slowly, his fingers drift up and over my shoulder, trailing down the strap of my lacy bra.

I bite my lip to stop myself from moaning.

Slowly, his fingertips glide down toward the place where the lace hugs my breast.

I can't look.

But I also can't look away.

"I wonder how much you'll pretend with me," he whispers. One of his fingertips skates right along the cup, getting perilously close to my nipple, which is poking through the lace at his touch.

"Pretend?" I repeat. Like a total idiot.

Marco's lips curl into a smile. "You want to pretend we're together. Pretend that you and I chose each other. That there was never a lie between us. What else will you have me pretend?" he purrs.

But the edge of his voice has turned hard.

I pull out of his grasp, panting as I spin and stare at him. "You said you'd help," I say.

He nods, tilting his head. "I did."

"So you need to help."

"I am."

I shut my eyes. "You're not."

Marco's voice is like silk. "I'm not?"

"No," I whisper. "Because Liam knows..."

I freeze.

Marco stands, his fabric-covered body rustling. "What about Liam?"

No point in telling him a lie. "Liam knows I'd never... date someone like you."

"And you know this how?"

My nostrils flare. I look Marco directly in the eye. "Because I hate mafia men, Marco. With every fiber of my being. So if you want to help, you're going to have to be someone else, or convince Liam that somehow I've changed my entire personality... for you."

6

MARCO

Her words are oddly shocking to me.

For one thing, Roisin is not just from 'a mafia family'. Her family is as old as mine when it comes to organized crime, and just as successful. She's absolutely not some kind of outlier, or someone who is adjacent to this world.

Her father is the MacAntyre that supplied the guns for part of the rebels in Ireland. They've been a part of Irish resistance for years.

Not for the cause, though. For a healthy, healthy paycheck.

The fact that she's staring up at me, her green eyes wide with rage, her hair wriggling out from the tight bun that she wrangled it into earlier, her cheeks flushed with rage…

I can see the blush of her anger, all the way down to the tops of her breasts.

Her breasts that are just begging for my touch.

When I came in to this dressing room, I expected to find her ready to go. I informed the shop attendants that it would be three hours and then I needed her, because we would be on the road to wherever Liam and Stassi are.

I didn't expect to find her...

In a state of undress.

It puts me right back to that night when I found out that she was a MacAntyre.

Right back to the moment where I first started to wonder what was truth, and what was a lie.

And with her current confession, we're right back there again.

I step back, my spine stiffening. "You hate mafia men?"

"With every fiber of my being," she spits.

Her accent is thicker now. It's rarely as pronounced as it is at the moment, and it's...

Fucking sexy.

I growl. I'm frustrated and I want to reach inside that fucking whisper of lace and tug out her pretty pale nipples, and rip the remaining fabric off of her body before trapping her in front of the mirror and slowly peeling the pants she's wearing off. I want to make her watch as I slide my fingers down and inside her...

Stop.

I take a deep breath, struggling to regain control. Shutting my eyes, I let it out, counting the beats as I exhale my fury into the crowded dressing room.

"Did you hate them when you decided to kiss me that day at the cottage?" I rasp.

Fucking hell.

I can't help myself, can I?

I seethe at my lack of control. I never get like this. I'm not Dino. Controlling my mouth, and my intentions, is a pivotal piece of my job.

More than that, I've been able to hide who I am from everyone. Always.

The fact that Roisin keeps digging my true self out from under all of these layers is...

Inconvenient.

She makes a small noise in her throat. "That was different."

My eyes fly open, and they search for hers. "How?"

Roisin looks away. "You... it's just different."

Something inside of me *snaps.*

In a heartbeat, I'm pushing Roisin up against the dressing room wall. Her eyes are wide and her strong arms are ready to grab me, but I gather both wrists in one hand and pin them up above her head. She pulls, and I'm impressed all over again at the strength in her slim body.

Unfortunately for her, I am stronger.

"You think I'm different? I'm not, Roisin. I'm every fucking inch a mafia boss. It's in my blood, and if you think for one second that I'm any fucking different, you're fucking fooling yourself," I snarl.

Roisin squirms, and one of my knees comes up to part her legs.

We realize that she's so wet she's practically dripping through both layers of clothing at exactly the same time.

Roisin blushes, turning her head. "Don't think this has anything to do with you," she snaps.

Oh.

That's how you want to play it, then?

"I think it has everything to do with me," I rumble, leaning forward until our faces are nearly pressed together. "In fact, I think if I put my hands inside... whatever the fuck this is, I think you'd be soaking wet for me, Rosin."

Her pupils go wide, and her lips part. She licks them, and her little pink tongue darting out makes my cock pulse painfully against my zipper.

"Jumpsuit."

I blink. "The fuck?"

"It's called a jump–"

I don't give a fuck.

I crash my lips over hers, because her voice is throaty and because when she spoke, she rubbed herself on my thigh.

She wants me.

I fucking know it.

Roisin leans into the kiss, her lips parting as my tongue slips inside. She moans, rubbing herself on my thigh as I drop her hands from mine and cup her face, deepening our kiss.

When I can feel her heat pulsing through the fabric of my trousers, I pull back and press my forehead to hers.

"Fuck, Roisin..."

"Do you want me or not?" she whispers.

I look down at her lips.

This is a very bad idea.

We're not supposed to do this. We're not supposed to have anything *real*.

And she just told me that she hates mafia men. Which I absolutely am. She said it with so much fire, it actually makes me feel like I'm going fucking crazy.

I know I must be, because I take one look at her beautiful green eyes.

And I decide.

I curl my hand up the back of her neck and grab a fistful of her beautiful strawberry blonde hair, pulling it out of the bun that she's fighting a losing battle against anyway. It feels like yards and yards of silk in my hand, the curls wrapping around my fingers, welcoming me in, and I tug her head back to get better access to her mouth.

She gasps.

And I'm gone.

I devour her. There's no other word for it. I've never kissed anyone like this, and I've never had a kiss like this.

Ever.

Even when we kissed at the cottage, it wasn't like *this*.

This is so much more than just a kiss. It's... an obsession. I'm lost in her. My hands roam her body, greedy to experience everything. The silk of her skin and the lace covering it make me crazy, because the difference in textures makes me want to use all my senses on her.

I want to feel how wet she is for me.

I want to taste her skin, taste the spot that's practically weeping onto my thigh.

I want to watch her, to see what she looks like when she comes, wrapped around me with her head thrown back, to watch my cock plunge into the sweet release of her body...

I want her. I want her so badly.

This kiss is more than it was before. More than the gentle exploration that we had of each other that day.

This is something unfinished. Something that we waited too long to address.

Something that's been burning us both up.

Roisin isn't protesting anymore. Her hands scrape against my neck, mussing the hair that I just worked so hard to get into shape. Without letting her lips move from mine, my hands circle under her hips and I lift.

She squeaks, but I wrap her legs around mine and press her into the mirror in front of us.

Every touch is a new treasure that I hoard to myself. Her skin is so soft when I free it from the clothes. *My* clothes, the ones that I bought for her.

The ones that she'll wear for me, if I want them.

I strip the wildly offensive lace bra from her body, tossing it behind me. I take a minute, panting, to take her in.

I scrape my hand over my mouth, trying to hide the hunger that I'm sure is practically radiating from my face. "Jesus, Roisin. You're fucking stunning," I murmur.

She blushes, looking away, but I continue to look at her.

Her hips curve out before dipping back into her neat waist. I lean forward, cupping her breasts in my hands, and her perfect soft flesh flows over the sides of my hands.

When I lick her pert pink nipples, she moans and its fucking music to my ears.

I want this.

I want this so badly it practically ripples through me.

Feasting on her nipples, I pluck and roll them until she's wiggling, her center rocking against me as she practically rubs herself against my cock.

"Fuck, Roisin," I growl. "You can't do that."

"Don't tell me what to do," she barks.

I grin.

I love this with her. It's never easy. She never backs down, she's never afraid of me.

However, in a second her fingertips are coasting along the edge of my pants, and I moan at the sensation.

We didn't make it this far, last time.

We didn't have the chance.

Her fingers in the waist of my pants feel cautious, but curious. When she wraps them around my hard cock, I have to take in a deep breath to keep myself from erupting.

I don't want to come like this.

I want to be inside her. I want to feel her wrapped around me. I want…

Dropping her abruptly, I move so that she's in front of me, and I'm behind her.

Roisin squirms, but I band an arm across her stomach, pinning her against me. In the mirror, I can see both of us, and the quaking of her breath as she breathes, staring at me in the mirror.

I want her. I want her so much.

My voice is practically guttural. "Do you want me to touch you, Roisin?"

She hesitates.

It's the hesitation that's going to kill me.

I hate mafia men.

Should I stop? Should I…

"Don't stop," she whispers.

Fucking hell, I can't.

With a growl, I span my hand across her waist and sink it slowly down against her skin, until I reach the spot where her… pelvic bone meets the curve of her hip.

I stop there, looking at her eyes in the mirror.

She nods.

My lips trace against the side of her neck, my eyes locked with hers as my fingers press against her skin, slowly smoothing down so that they're coasting over the smooth, firm skin of her belly.

"Fuck, Roisin," I groan as my fingertips reach the center of her heat. "You're so fucking wet for me."

I expect her to disagree, to say something like she's not, or it's not for me.

Instead, she shocks the hell out of me by gasping, "Yes."

I bite at the column of her neck. 'Do you need to come, baby?"

Her eyes roll back in her head and she moans.

I take that as a yes.

Slowly, I slip a finger inside of her, utterly shocked at the amount of moisture gathered there. Roisin's knees buckle, and I hold her tighter. She's propped up by my fingers inside her and my arm banded under her breasts, and the sight of her in the mirror, my hand working the thin fabric of her panties as I slide in and out of her, is the most erotic thing I've ever seen.

She shudders, and I smile.

She's close.

"Come for me, Roisin," I whisper against her ear. "Be a good girl and come all over my hand. Let me see how fucking much you want me, and come for me–"

I meant to say more. Clearly, she likes it when I talk dirty to her though, because I don't have to say anything else.

Roisin explodes on my hand.

There's no other way to describe it. I feel her muscles ripple as they tug my fingers deeply inside, and she gasps as she throws her head back. Watching her shake, while my fingers are embedded in her...

It takes every single fiber of my being to keep myself from coming in my pants.

When her body stops shuddering and her eyes don't look quite so glazed, I gently pull my fingers out of her. In the mirror, I catch her gaze and lift the fingers to my mouth.

Slowly, I lick her from my fingertips, and I watch with satisfaction as her nipples tighten again and her mouth parts.

"You may hate mafia men, Roisin, but I just made you come apart with my fingertips. Hate me all you want... but just know that you fucking shattered. For me," I growl.

With that, I slam the dressing room door open and stalk out.

Leaving Roisin behind.

A solid hour later, which I'm sure she decided to do out of spite, and Roisin is heading for the front of the department store.

She looks amazing.

She's wearing the most expensive athletic pants that I've ever seen, and they sculpt her toned body into looking like a fitness model. I swear I can see every muscle in her legs flex as she walks, and the expensive-looking bra top cups her breasts so perfectly, I ache to reach out and touch them.

She managed to wrangle her strawberry curls into two long braids, and despite the fact that she looks cute as a button in them, I know that they're not meant to be attractive.

Roisin didn't dress like I am expecting her to, and she knows it.

She dressed for war.

My blood heats. I can't tell if she knows what she's doing to me or not, but fuck me.

I love a fucking challenge.

She tugs on an athletic jacket. "I'm ready," she practically snaps at me.

I raise an eyebrow. "Did you decide on something to bring?"

Instead of responding, Roisin just snaps her fingers. A small train of attendants rolls out of the women's dressing room area, each one of them rolling a suitcase that is probably chock-full of clothing, and each one with an expensive logo that I would be worried about hurting my credit card.

If I worried about such things.

I've been making investments through the years. I'm proud to say that it's my own, not tied to the family... before he went to jail, my grandfather gave me a gift of a thousand dollars.

I turned that into a portfolio that means I'll never have to worry about who is putting clothes on my credit card.

It's the only thing that I've really done for myself, or for a family that I had, in a fit of delusion, thought I might have one day.

The second my father died, though, that illusion was shattered for me.

Quickly.

I knew at that moment that I wouldn't ever be looking out for my own happiness in life.

I'd always be trying to figure out how to help my siblings. I'd always be watching over the family.

I took on the role of their protector, and I was happy to fill it.

But it did mean that my dream, and the assets I'd put together to live it, disappeared.

She glares at me. "I finished my shopping, *darling*."

The venom on the endearment makes me chuckle. "Well I hope it was worth your while, pumpkin."

"Oh, sweetheart, I certainly hope you meant it when you said this card had no limit."

At this point, the shop attendants are watching us like a tennis match. Aware of their attention, and the fact that they might be reporting to people who care about this, I move over to Roisin and tuck her close.

"You couldn't bankrupt me if you tried," I whisper.

She stiffens. "I'll see about that," she mutters.

Roisin peels away from me, stomping forward.

And I grin as her ass jiggles on the way out.

CHAPTER 6: ROISIN

I am the dumbest person alive.

In the Jaguar, Marco follows my directions. The back is stacked with an unseemly amount of packaging that jostles, rolling from side to side as we careen down the narrow Irish countryside, heading for our family home near Sligo.

I think that's where Liam is.

The fact that he appeared to me at the cottage recently does give me some doubt, but if he's getting married and trying to make at least somewhat of a spectacle of it, then he's going to be at home in the house that's officially unofficial.

As it always has to be.

I meant what I said to Marco in the dressing room. I do hate mafia men. I hate that they're bossy and demanding, that they think you owe them every single thing.

I hate that they're self-assured and conceited. That they think you can throw money at a problem and it will all go away.

I hate how much they're like my father, if I'm being honest.

The problem is that Marco?

He's nothing like my father.

My fingers drum anxiously on the leather interior, the luxury of it absorbing the sound from my fingertips annoyingly well.

Marco is...

In many ways, yes. He's absolutely a mafia man. He's conniving and arrogant and slick, always with a plan up his sleeve and a fucking song in his heart as he murders people in cold blood.

I've seen him do it.

But on the other hand..

The Marco that I got to know at the cottage is kind. He's protective, but in a way that doesn't feel condescending or overbearing. I had the sense, many times, that he genuinely cared for me.

That he wanted me.

Just like I wanted him.

Just like you still want him, you hussy.

I flush.

The memory of riding Marco's thigh, and then his fingers, is something that I'm probably going to feel very conflicted about for a long time. Because, as much as I hate to admit it, I want Marco with every fiber of my being.

Which is a problem in itself.

I promised myself a very long time ago that I wouldn't sleep with anyone who was in the same sphere of influence as my brothers and my dad. After Kieran scared the shit out of me, and my dad basically imprisoned me, I swore off men altogether.

You'll find someone you want badly enough to try all this out with, I would tell myself.

I know the basics. I own a vibrator, and I'm not naive or anything.

But the truth is, I haven't exactly been with a man yet.

And that... almost went out the window earlier today, when I was practically begging Marco to take me.

I shuffle, uncomfortable as I look out the window.

The Jaguar is literally eating up the road on the way to Sligo. The family home, interestingly, is an old converted manor. The joke was that the English lord who tried to inhabit it was killed because of MacAntyre weapons that we smuggled into the country back in the day, so it was given to the MacAntyre family.

Except it isn't in our family name.

The people in the town protect us, which is something that I've hated ever since I was a child. I can see how for Liam it's an advantage right now, and it's another reason I'm thinking he will probably have the wedding here. He can control, through the town, who has access to our home.

When I was a child, though?

I wanted to escape from my father. I wanted to find my mother again, to figure out where he and Kieran had hidden her. I tried to walk away more times than I can count, and every time it was a well-meaning, if wayward, townsperson who brought me back, kicking and screaming, to my father's house.

The memory makes me shiver.

I don't like mafia men. I don't. My reasons are my own and they're perfectly rational. Who would, after everything I've been through?

But the memory of Marco's hands on my body lingers.

"So. What's the story?" Marco rumbles.

I shift, staring at him.

He winks. "What are we going to tell them about how we met?"

"The exact story about how we met. I took you into custody—"

"Won't work," Marco shakes his head. "They're going to know that I chose to be in custody."

I snort. "You didn't say that when I had you at gunpoint. It seemed you were very much at my mercy then."

"You'd love to think that, wouldn't you Roisin?"

I arch my eyebrow at him. "You were allowing yourself to be caught?"

He nods. "Yes."

"Why the hell would you do that?'

"So that I could negotiate the deal to protect Dino's children," he says without skipping a beat.

I blink. "We offered you that deal–"

"I knew you would, as soon as I heard that Interpol had located the twins and Marisol. Dino came to me to ask me what to do years ago. I monitored them. It only happened recently that they were on Interpol's radar, and I had to protect them."

My eyebrows knit together. If that's true, that means Marco...

"You just... stayed in witness protection?"

"Yes."

I shake my head. "Why?"

Marco sighs. "Because I needed to at the time."

"That's ludicrous."

"It's what we mafia men do to protect what's ours," he says in a voice that feels laced with venom and promise.

Hmm. Interesting. Clearly, my comment earlier bothered him. "You'd just as easily sell him out if you had to," I say quietly.

Marco's hands tighten on the steering wheel, but he doesn't respond.

We continue in silence, as we wind up the road. Eventually, a familiar bend comes up, and my heart aches as the manor house comes into view.

"Welcome to Aughris House, Marco," I say quietly.

My heart sinks.

Because this house is my worst fucking nightmare.

I kind of want to ask Marco what he's thinking as we walk up the stone drive to the house.

Kind of.

But not really, because I'm currently refusing to speak to him until otherwise indicated.

That, of course, and I don't really want to be here so…

Silence dominates our conversation.

The house isn't huge. On the outside, it looks like a lot of other old houses in Ireland. Stone walls covered in whitewash, two stories and several wings, and the type of old-fashioned peaked roof that has to have a specialist come in to repair. It's bigger than some manor houses around the area, built a little more like a castle than just a house, but it's not exactly out of the ordinary.

Except for the roses.

The entire structure is nearly covered in climbing roses, and a garden of roses winds around it for what feels like a mile. Even now, in the early part of the year, walking up to it is impressive. There aren't many in bloom right now, except for some of the smaller, hardier winter ones, but in the summer the whole thing is basically covered in blooms.

Behind me, Marco makes a noise.

I turn. "What."

"That is an insane amount of roses."

I could tell him that it's how I got my name. My mother was so impressed by being brought back here, before she knew what my father was, that she named me for the roses on the house. There's always been a girl in the family who bears the name of the roses.

My father was thrilled, of course, when I could take that one.

And furious when she stole me away and hid me from him.

Furious enough that he basically burned things down to find me again… and my mom hasn't' been seen since.

The thought makes anger burn through me, so instead of responding to Marco I turn on my heel and march to the front door. Unfortunately, that means that I'm once again face-to-face with the manor house.

Ugh.

It really should be gorgeous. The roses and the stone walls, with whatever chemical is on them to make them white, are a shocking contrast. It makes the vines of the roses almost look black, and without the brilliant blooms, the whole effect is kind of like a goth house. Behind the house, I can just see the edge of the pond that comes with the property. I know that if

I keep walking in that direction, I'll come across a stable where my father kept all his prized horses.

Further on, I'd find myself on a path to the sea. The Atlantic Ocean is brutal on this side of Ireland, nothing like the deep (if narrow) Irish channel. On this side of the country, the sea stretches like an endless line on the horizon.

I used to think that I could see New York, if I tried hard enough.

Until Kieran almost drowned me by shoving me down the cliffs into the freezing ocean below. He disavowed me of that belief, by pointing out how stupid I was to think that you can see America from Ireland.

Most of my memories of this beautiful place are, in fact, completely ruined by Kieran.

I wish the dread that's threading through me at the thought of seeing his twin wasn't so total. Liam technically never did any of those things to me that Kieran did.

Technically.

Still, it's insanely hard to look someone wearing the same face as the one that comes straight from your nightmares in the eyes, and believe that he won't hurt you.

I know it bothers Liam. It's probably the only reason that he maintains our little spying arrangement. I'm sure if I just stopped giving him information, he wouldn't ask why.

But, he seems to use it to his advantage.

I'm still not sure why I do it. Family loyalty. Terror of my brother's ghost.

Mostly, just a connection to keep to my family, in case he hears anything about my mother that I wouldn't hear through Interpol, I guess.

This is all so fucked up.

"Roisin?"

Marco must have noticed that I'm at a dead stop on the path, glaring up at the house. I don't answer him. Instead, I march forward until we're on the threshold, feet poised to take the step up into the ancient home.

I'm surprised there's not a security guard or something outside... or maybe there are, and I just haven't noticed.

I crane my head up and grimace.

Yep. Someone's sitting on the roof with a rifle aimed down at us.

Resisting the urge to yell that I do, in fact, live here, I go to knock on the door...

Only to find it's already swinging open.

I blink, my hand raised in front of the thick carved wood panel in front of me.

"Ro?"

I let myself smile, the movement kind of rusty. "Hi Liam."

"What are you doing here?" my brother asks.

He hasn't noticed Marco yet. I can't decide if that's a good thing or a bad thing. "I came for the wedding."

"The wedding isn't for a few weeks..."

"Good," I murmur. I'm curious if Stassi is here, because if she is, I want to look at her. I want to make sure that Liam isn't doing the thing that Kieran would do.

Which is to say... I want to make sure that he's not kidnapping her and forcing her to be here.

I can tell the moment Liam notices Marco. His easy going demeanor shifts, and all of a sudden there's someone in front of me who doesn't look like Liam at all.

My fists clench. He looks like Kieran.

Kieran is dead.

"Who's this then?" Liam rumbles.

Marco steps forward, gently putting his hand over my shoulder. "Marco De Luca."

"I know who you are. The fuck are you doing here with my sister?"

I know Marco will have an answer.

I'm sure it's not the answer I want.

So, before he can get it out, I toss his hand out of the way and look at Liam.

"Marco's here to be my wedding date."

7

MARCO

If it wasn't so important for him to believe us, I'd laugh out loud at the look on Liam MacAntyre's face.

It's shock. Pure and simple.

The kind of shock that tells me he not only had no idea, but the whole thing is completely and utterly absurd to him.

Again, if Roisin didn't need him to believe it in order to clear her name…

Yeah. It would be pretty fucking funny. It's rare to pull one over on a guy like this, and Liam MacAntyre, unlike his brother, appears to be both smart and relatively aware of all the shit going on around him.

But he couldn't have had any idea that this was coming.

Neither did I, as it were.

"Liam?" Roisin's voice is uncharacteristically small. It makes me shuffle, and before I realize what I'm doing, I catch myself trying to stand in front of her.

Like I'm going to protect her.

From her own brother.

The fuck are you doing?

Liam blinks, shaking his head like a dog. "Sorry. I could have sworn you just said that Marco De Luca is here as your date. To my wedding."

Roisin straightens a little, the iron that I'm used to seeing etching her posture. "That's because I did."

"But..." Liam trails off. He glances between us.

I see the moment something clicks for him.

"Well then De Luca, I guess the mystery of where you've been for the past fucking year is solved."

"My family was aware of my whereabouts," I say softly.

Liam's eyebrows raise. "I think they were not."

"Would it be any of your business?" I say sharply.

Liam's nostrils flare, and I can see his eyes, which look so much like Roisin's, darken with anger.

It's true. It wouldn't be his business. His brother, Kieran, had tried to kidnap my sister. Kieran also tried to kill my niece, and I was so hell-bent on proving Elio guilty for the murder of my parents that I never fucking saw it coming.

The thought of the whole situation, and my own blindness in everything that happened back then, makes me shiver with rage at myself. To this day, that span of time is one of the worst things that has ever happened to me.

And it was even worse for Caterina.

I still thank God for Gia and Elio, who were able to quickly figure out where she was and saved her.

Because I was too fucking adamant that Elio had killed my parents to admit that he hadn't. And, in the process, I'd made more enemies in the form of the Irish.

To this day, we're still on shaky ground. Liam is a much, much better man that Kieran was, in terms of his general sanity.

However, that doesn't make him happy to see me, by any means.

I force myself to crack a smile. "Roisin and I met while she had me in custody."

"So you know, then," he rasps.

Interesting. His voice carries the same protective note that mine often does when I talk about my siblings.

I tilt my head. From what I remember, Liam didn't grow up with Kieran and Roisin. He had an uncle or something who took him. Maybe the birth mom, I can't remember.

But I'm going to figure it out right fucking quick.

"I know that Roisin works for Interpol. Something that I imagine Interpol doesn't necessarily want to know."

"Aye," Liam interrupts. "And the fucker who tattles on her— "

"I quit," Roisin blurts.

We both look at her.

She sighs, and the breath she takes conveys so much weariness that I resist the urge to step next to her and wrap my arms around her shoulders.

"I quit working for Interpol. It was just too hard. I couldn't... lie to them anymore," she manages.

Liam's lips thin into a hard line. "You didn't want to tell me the last time I saw you, then?"

"No," she says sharply.

"It was just—"

"I said no. I wasn't ready to tell you then, and when I heard about you getting married, I wanted to come. To welcome Stassi into the family," she says.

I don't miss the way she cut him off. *When did he last come by?*

And why?

Liam's eyes narrow. "How did you know she goes by Stassi?"

"She's literally a world-famous model, Liam. Congrats on that too, by the way," I drawl.

Stassi has a PhD in physics too, but she likes to keep that under wraps, if memory serves. It makes her significantly more dangerous than anyone realizes.

Which is another reason I agreed to this whole song and dance.

Anastasia Novikov doesn't do anything anyone tells her to without very, very good reason.

There is no way she would have agreed with Elio to marry Liam to neutralize the Irish threat without some kind of plan. Liam had kidnapped Gia, my sister-in-law and Elio's twin, to try and forge some kind of alliance between the organizations. Kieran, shockingly, was a terrible leader who practically drove the Irish organization into bankruptcy, a dangerous thing when there are no banks and people come looking for their pound of flesh when they don't get their cash. Gia was pregnant with my brother Sal's baby when Liam kidnapped her, in order to get some kind of financial backing from Elio.

But Stassi stepped in and volunteered to marry him.

For some unknown reason.

And I want to know what it is.

Because if she has any intention of using her newfound power to hurt my family...

Liam grunts, pulling my attention. "So you're just here for the wedding."

"Yes," Roisin says.

"That's several weeks away."

She shrugs. "Figured my new sister could use someone around to do all the girly things with her."

Liam barks a laugh, earning a strange glance from both Roisin and I.

"Something funny about that, brother?" she says.

He shakes his head and opens the door. "You'll see."

Roisin goes in, her shoulders relaxing slightly as she passes the threshold to the door. I hesitate just a second, then follow her.

But not before a large hand presses on my shoulder.

I stop, eye-level with Liam.

He studies me. This close, I can see the bags under his eyes, and the darkness against the edges of his lips.

Liam isn't fucking happy about this.

In fact, I'd say the opposite is true.

"I don't know what your fucking game is, De Luca," he says under his breath, "but if you fucking touch one hair on my sister's head, all bets are off."

"What bets?" I say, the picture of innocence.

His lips press into a line, and he lets out a growl. "I'll fucking show you how deep the crazy runs in this family, you bastard. That's the fucking bet. You think Kieran and I are different? We're fucking not. The only difference is that I can keep my leash on, and he never could."

Now *that* is fascinating.

I tilt my head and give him a smile, then clap him on the shoulder. "I look forward to spending time with you, Liam. It's always nice to know more about Roisin and where she comes from," I smirk.

Liam's nostrils flare and I know I've hit a sore spot.

I hear female voices from further inside the house, and I brush off Liam's shoulder, following them in.

Despite the fact that I'm supposed to be here to help Roisin, I find that I'm intrigued all around.

Something is rotten in this house. Something is strange about why Stassi, who can have literally anyone she wants, would choose to shackle herself to Liam.

The game has changed. I'm no longer here to help Roisin, which I never really wanted in the first place.

I'm going to do what I do best.

Figure out how to protect my fucking family.

At all fucking costs.

I follow the sound of Roisin and Stassi's voices as they echo down the hall, noting the details of the house as I go. I'm no stranger to family homes that carry a lot of history. Supposedly there's a De Luca estate in Italy still, but I've never been.

I have, however, been to Elio's family home in Italy. Fucking stunning. I went when I was in college, and he was there learning the ropes from his dad, a real old-school Italian who had a dark, booming laugh and more than a few raunchy stories always ready to tell.

For a minute, my memory clouds. I remember being so jealous of their relationship. My father was… harder. I never quite knew why, but some of the documents that I found after his death gave me some kind of clue about what might have hardened him.

Including the fact that my mother had an affair.

Including the fact that his father, and his uncles, were all sent to jail in the 80s on bullshit RICO charges, and they left him to run the business alone.

His journal, which I found nearly a week after their deaths, as well as my mother's journals, all told a story that I had never heard, but explained a lot.

However, a child should not know those things about their parents. After they died, and I couldn't ask any questions?

It was too fucking much.

"Oh my god. This looks incredible," I hear Roisin breathe.

Blinking, I take myself back to the present.

And I find myself in a fucking sea of white lace and pearls.

I look around the room, my eyebrows winging up as I do.

There are wedding dresses... everywhere.

We're in some kind of parlor room, by the looks of it. It's quite typical of a British Isles parlor room, with wood detailing on all the walls, wood floors covered by antique Persian rugs, and all kinds of pictures, trinkets, and other shit covering every available surface. There's a piano, which I find somewhat unusual, and a large portrait of a beautiful woman hanging over the fireplace.

And wedding dresses.

I'm momentarily stunned.

Roisin makes a noise again, pulling my attention to the center of the room, where there's a large tri-fold mirror set up to catch the light from the large windows. A changing screen, very old-fashioned looking, is connected to it, and there are even more wedding dresses frothing the top of the screen.

Behind it, I see the shape of a woman, and I automatically avert my eyes.

I'm not trying to see Stassi naked.

"Well, I like couldn't decide on any dress and with the tight timeline there just aren't that many places to do the tailoring," Stassi says from behind the screen, "so I just like... bought them all."

I blink.

Liam, finally coming up behind me from the hall, makes a noise. "Anastasia. We have... visitors."

I glance into the room, watching Roisin as she walks from dress to dress, her fingers lingering on the fabric. The reverential way that she's touching each one makes something in my chest hurt.

Does she... want to get married?

Fuck.

Movement catches my eye, and Anastasia pokes her head out from behind the screen. She beams at Liam. "I know! Your sister, Roisin! Why didn't you tell me she was coming?"

She ducks back behind the screen. "Wait! Liam, you can't like, come in!"

Liam, to my surprise, seems to look a little embarrassed. "It's not like any of those things matter—"

"You want to jinx our marriage! Oh my god, Liam, are you for real?"

Stassi's California-style accent is actually entertaining. Not for the first time, I wonder what her dissertation defense was like, and whether it went something along the lines of "Like, this is totally my physics dissertation."

Roisin turns to us, her eyes twinkling with genuine laughter. For a second, the look on her face freezes me in my tracks.

God, she's fucking pretty when she's happy.

Then, she flaps her hands, shooing us from the room. "Go. Get my bags and do man things. We're good here," she says.

Then, with a very final click, the doors to the parlor snap closed.

Leaving Liam and I befuddled and a little overwhelmed, scratching our heads in the hallway.

8

ROISIN

I HAVE TO ADMIT.

Stassi Novikov is... fun.

The second I walked into the ladies' parlor, she came after me like a tulle-encrusted whirlwind. I was instantly hugged, kissed on both cheeks, and sat down with a glass of champagne before I even knew what was going on.

For the first time in days, weeks, or maybe even months, I felt a glimmer of... fun.

I wasn't about to let my stupid brother and Marco ruin that for me.

So I took full advantage of Stassi's squeak about the tradition of not seeing the bride in her dress before the wedding.

And when I snapped the parlor doors shut, I wanted to laugh out loud at the looks on their faces.

"Wait until they're gone and then come try one of these on with me," Stassi said from the center of the room.

I press my ear against the door, then grin at her after a minute. "They're gone."

"Good," she says with a bright smile. The dress she has on looks like it was made by spiders or something, the lace is so finely made and stretched over a tight white silk under-dress.

She stands, reaching for the bottle of champagne, and I sigh.

Stassi turns back, her perfect rose lips arched in a little catlike smile. "Here, new sister."

"Thanks," I say, accepting the drink.

We both sip, and I sigh. "Wow. That's amazing."

"I know. They send me this stuff by the case, and I just honestly never drink it. But when I do," she sips, her perfect blue eyes closing in admiration. "It's like... really good."

I take another drink.

"So. Which one do you want to try?"

I look at Stassi. She's literally a model; she's tall, with elegantly long limbs and the type of blonde hair that turns nearly white in the summer. Her skin still carries the tan of whatever exotic location she was last in, and she has the kind of body that most of us only dream of.

"Uh," I start. "I hate to tell you this, but I don't think you and I wear the same size."

She laughs. "Oh my god, girl. Don't worry about it. They make wedding dresses too big so that you can get them tailored."

I eye her very trim waist. "I'm not sure..."

"Just come on, already. You can totally pick one, I promise you'll fit!"

Before I know it, Stassi's hand is in mine, and I'm being pulled toward one of the racks of wedding dresses at an alarmingly quick pace.

I dig in my heels, preventing the champagne from spilling. "Look," I protest, "I'm not even sure where to start—"

"Sweetheart neckline," she says, thrusting a dress at me.

I blink. "What?"

"Sweetheart neckline. You've got killer bone structure on your shoulders and along your collarbones, so let's go with this," she smiles.

I don't know how anyone says no to this woman.

With a sigh, I grab the dress and hand her my champagne. Behind the screen, I whip off the well-made designer jumpsuit that I was wearing, my fingers lingering on the edges of the lingerie that I still haven't changed out of.

The lingerie that Marco...

"So. Tell me about yourself, Roisin?"

I wince.

I don't know what to do. Stassi just seems so... open. I don't want to lie to her, but I can't tell her the truth.

I don't even think that I know how to answer that question. My brain sifts through the different layers of the truth as I try to figure out what I'm going for.

I'm an Interpol agent being framed for the murder of Russian mafia members. You might know them.

I'm a double agent, working for Interpol to arrest members of organized crime while also feeding my brother information that keeps our stupid family gang afloat.

I'm Marco's handler, and held him in witness protection for almost a year.

I'm...

"Oh I know! Tell me what your color season is!"

That makes me pause.

Then, I huff a little laugh.

Of course she doesn't want you to go that deep. She doesn't even know you.

"I don't know what that is," I call as I tug the dress up. I have to admit, even though it doesn't quite lace up in the back, it makes my tits look amazing. For a second, I study myself in the mirror.

She's not wrong. I look... really good.

The bodice of the gown curves around me in a way that's somehow both classy and alluring. It's a shimmery, buttery-looking fabric. Satin, I think, but I could be wrong. Might be silk or who knows what else.

Magic. It has to be made of magic.

"Don't be shy! Do you have it on? Let me see!" Stassi says from the center of the room.

I take a deep breath and step out from behind the screen. Stassi is waiting next to the mirror and the little pedestal is right in front of her, smack in the middle where you'd be able to see yourself from all angles.

She waves, pointing to the pedestal. "Step up!"

Hesitating, I do.

When I get up, I don't want to look at myself in the mirror. Stassi appears behind me, and with a few quick tugs and what looks like some kind of clamp, the dress somehow glues itself to my frame.

"Oh. My. God. Roisin. You have to open your eyes," she breathes.

Slowly, I open one.

Stassi and I both gasp at my reflection.

"Holy mother of god," I breathe, smoothing the fabric over myself. "I look—"

"Freaking incredible!" Stassi trills.

I do.

This dress transforms all my muscles into something elegant and feminine. I look like I've been sculpted from marble or something.

And Stassi, a golden goddess, just beams behind me.

"Okay. Now I see why you have so many dresses," I breathe. I've never really spent time trying wedding dresses on, for obvious reasons, but I can sure see why this would be fun.

I look amazing.

Stassi grins. "Totally. I want to make sure that Liam has absolutely no clue what I'm going to wear."

"Oh, he was never going to have a single bloody idea," I murmur, tracing the fabric over my thighs.

Stassi grins. "It's good to make him sweat a little though."

I catch her gaze. "Absolutely. And he bought all of these?" I wave around.

Stassi rolls her eyes. "I'm not that cruel. It's obvious that he wants me for my money and all that I come with. That's why Kieran kidnapped me."

I turn, ripping my eyes away from the mirror and staring at her. "What?"

Stassi's smile falters slightly. "You didn't know?"

"No. Please tell me," I say.

She tugs me to the stiff couch. With her hands flitting like birds, punctuating her statements, she starts.

By the time Stassi is done, there's a knot of rage and sorrow in my chest that feels like it's blocking my air supply.

I take a deep breath, trying to calm myself down enough to get around it. "Lord have mercy, Stassi," I breathe. "I'm so fuckin' sorry."

Her demeanor, which has been fairly sunny until now, droops slightly. "It wasn't your fault."

There, of course, is the problem.

"It might not be my fault, but I still wish it hadn't happened to you," I mutter. *And I'm still related to the motherfucker who did it.*

It's never my fault.

But I'm still responsible.

Stassi's face hardens. For a second, the bubbly California girl disappears, and I see a glint of something much, much more serious in her eyes.

"It's not your fault," she repeats, this time with steel coming through her voice. "I need you to know that."

"I know."

"No," she shakes her head. "I don't think you do. I think you're doing the exact same thing that I do, in situations like this. But you aren't responsible for the things your brother, or brothers, do."

My eyes flick to hers. "Brothers?"

I swear to God, if Liam…

"Well. I guess I opted in to one brother. I just didn't choose the other one," she says with a smile that's way too sad.

"Stassi…"

She waves a hand, cutting off my weak attempt at reassurance. "I'm a Novikov, Roisin. I understand what it means to live in a world where my family, and the sins of my relatives, are my own. That's why I need you to know. It's not your fault," she says.

There's so much conviction in her voice. I want to protest, but as she stares at me in the mirror, I recognize that she's not just telling me it's not my fault.

She's telling herself that as well.

I take a deep breath, meeting her gaze. I crack a smile and give her a wink.

"I think you should probably call me Ro, since you're going to be my sister in less than thirty days."

The smile that blooms across Stassi's face isn't manufactured in the slightest. It's genuine, beautiful, and it warms me to my core.

"I always wanted a sister," she says with a smile.

I nod.

Because. While I never particularly wanted a sister, I'm sure glad to have one now.

There are a great deal of dresses.

And a lot of champagne.

And, by the time that we've gone through the whole room, I am well and truly drunk.

Stassi, normal, bubbly Stassi, is back. She's hilarious, and I collapse back at her latest joke, melting into the puddle of lace and stiff tulle that comprises the princess-style dress I have on.

"Stop," I breathe, struggling to keep my champagne glass upright as I fight my way out of the fabric puddling around me. "There's no way that you were there the night that Megan met Harry."

She winks, her cheeks flush with champagne. "Who do you think told her to go for it?"

"The news always reported they met through friends," I giggle.

Stassi smiles. "Am I not a friend?"

I have no doubt that Stassi is the best friend in the world.

"Far be it from me to interject," I hear my brother's voice ring into the room.

Stassi giggles. "He won't come in. He's terrified."

"What, Liam?" I yell.

"Perhaps you'd like to eat something?" Liam says.

I roll my eyes, looking at Stassi. "Should I tell him to fuck off?" I whisper.

She wrinkles her nose. "Oh, we've probably made them suffer for long enough, right?"

My stomach grumbles, and I sigh. "I could eat."

"Coming, darling," Stassi trills.

I prop myself up so that I can see the doorway. Liam's face peers in, and sure enough, he toes the threshold but refuses to cross it.

Big baby.

Stassi sails out, dressed in only her silky robe. I watch her go, then sigh.

I should probably try to get up.

The dress, however, is a problem. There's just so *much* of it. And, I need to manage to get up without spilling any of that champagne that's making my head spin. I eye the floor, then my hand, then make one attempt.

Shit.

Attempt number two is almost successful. I'm partly standing when I almost lose my balance again. The vision of the champagne flying through the air and staining the perfectly pristine white dress enters my mind, and I squeak as I wait...

Then, strong hands cross my middle.

"Need a hand?" Marco says, his voice thick.

I blink.

Marco is behind me, slowly propping me up. I let him, feeling his hands at my waist like a burning brand.

By the time I'm standing, my face feels hot, and I bring myself to look in the mirror in front of us.

"This is... a lot," Marco rumbles.

My gaze snaps to his. "I'm allowed to wear dresses," I blurt.

Marco's eyes pull away from mine in the mirror. The heat that's blistering my cheeks spreads as his eyes slip down, over my neck and shoulders. This dress is a true princess-style dress, with a fitted strapless bodice and a skirt that puffs out for miles in any direction.

His eyes snag on the corset top, which is shoving my breasts up into actual cleavage.

"This part I like," he murmurs.

I'm too stunned to speak.

His hand tugs at the voluminous skirt. "This part is a lot."

"I can wear whatever I want," I protest.

Weakly.

Marco's eyes lock with mine again. "You can."

"If I want to get married," I whisper.

His eyes go dark. "Do you?"

I don't know. I don't know that I've ever given it too much thought, until now.

But the thought of Marco, standing there at the end of a long aisle, suddenly flashes into my mind.

"I might," I say, my voice hoarse.

His nostrils flare, and I can see the muscle in his jaw flex. The silence between us gets tense, like a bow string as it's pulled back to the tightest point.

Marco gives me one last, lingering look. "This isn't the one," he mutters.

With that, he spins, leaving the room.

I'm stunned.

Because he left right as another question popped into my mind.

Was he talking about the dress?

Or me?

9

MARCO

Fucking. Hell.

Seeing Roisin in that dress did something to me. It broke something that I didn't know existed. It created a loop, an endless cycle, that I can't seem to stop seeing.

The dress was hideous. Truly ugly, a frothy monstrosity that would have looked disturbingly inelegant on anyone...

Except Roisin.

She was stunning.

The delicate arch of her collarbone, the way the top was tight enough to press her luscious breasts up, creating an eye-catching amount of flesh that just begged for my touch, the neat waistline and how I could practically feel the arch of her hip under the voluminous fabric... she looked absolutely incredible in that fucking dress.

And, more than that, she looked like a *bride.*

Deep down, I am a possessive man. I want to protect the people I love, I want to make sure that they are happy, and I want it because they're *mine*.

When I saw Roisin in that dress, something clicked in my mind. She was no longer just Roisin.

She became *mine*.

The feeling was so sudden, it rattled me to my core. I stormed away before I did something ridiculous... like kiss her.

Touch her.

Rip the fucking dress off and fuck her in the middle of Liam's sitting room, which has been transformed by the ebullient Stassi Novikov into some kind of wedding planning headquarters.

Or a dress factory. I'm not sure which.

Either way, I couldn't fuck Roisin senseless in the middle of it.

So I left.

Now, though, we're sitting next to each other at the dinner table, which is oddly intimate. Liam and Stassi are sitting across from us, making this some kind of horribly fucked-up double date.

Even more so because Stassi is basically driving the entire conversation, and the rest of us are nodding along, caught in the torrent of her personality like fucking whitewater rafts in a spring torrent.

I force myself to focus on her words, and not on Roisin sitting next to me.

Stassi grabs some salad and passes the bowl to Liam. "Well that brings us to the flowers. Next, I'm thinking that we need some kind of options for the bar. Obviously an open bar—"

"For who?" Liam says.

Stassi arches an eyebrow. "Our guests."

"Were we planning on guests?" Liam mutters.

Stassi rolls her eyes. "Well I'm obviously inviting everyone that needs to be here in order for it to be legit."

"If we invite more than just the people in this room, we're going to risk something that can't be risked," Liam grunts.

That's interesting to me. "Risking what, exactly?"

Liam gives me a very wary stare, and I smile. "We're about to be family, MacAntyre . I can help."

"I need your help like I need a fuckin' bullet in my head," Liam retorts. "It's no secret that you're a fuckin' viper, De Luca. I'd prefer to not be bitten."

I've earned that, I guess. I put up my hands in a gesture of surrender. "All I'm saying is that there's a whole lot that I can contribute to the situation, and you may or may not be in a position to decline that help. I don't know your problems, but I do know that since Roisin is your sister, I'll lump you in as family."

His eyes narrow, and I lean back. "I might be a snake, but you sure as hell fuckin' know that it's to help my family."

I'm dead serious, and the severity of my tone seems to convey enough that Liam nods slightly.

Stassi taps one surprisingly sharp-looking nail against her glass. "So the guest list can expand?"

"Who the... hell do you want to bring?" Liam bites out.

Her eyes narrow. "My mother, for one."

"Stassi—"

"She knows I'd never get married without her. And if you don't want this whole thing to blow up in your face, you're going to need to have her on your side," she says.

The bubbly, California-girl accent is gone.

Interesting.

Liam looks at her for a minute, the bags under his eyes seemingly growing deeper by the second. Abruptly, he stands, the screech of the chair harsh as he backs out of the room.

We watch him go. Stassi sighs and looks at Roisin. "He literally runs every time I try to talk to him about something deeper than the weather."

"Liam's... Liam," Roisin offers lamely.

I lean in.

She gives me a wary look before shrugging. "We weren't raised together. I don't know where he gets it from. His mom was protected because she's too high-profile to hurt, and she was able to raise him separately as part of the divorce agreement."

"Divorce?" Stassi says, her eyebrows pinched together. "Divorce doesn't happen in our world."

"For her, it did. She and Niall, our father, had one. He raised Kieran. She raised Liam."

"Splitting up brothers is brutal," I mutter.

I'm surprised at how quickly the truth falls out of my mouth.

Both Stassi and Roisin turn to me.

I shrug. "I have two brothers. And a sister. I've been through a lot with them," I offer.

It's the tip of the iceberg. I would die for them.

I always planned to die for them.

When did that become past tense?

"Wait, but you didn't live with your dad?" Stassi is looking at Roisin again.

Roisin's shoulders slump, and I fight the urge to reach for her.

"No. I lived with my mom. Until my dad found us. Until Kieran found us," she whispers.

If I could kill that motherfucker a million times, I would.

The sorrow that's painted across her features makes something feral inside of me rise up and snarl with frustration. I want to destroy things, just to change that pain into something else.

I'm so riled up, I don't know how to fucking calm down. It takes everything in me to take deep breaths and try to keep my shit together.

You need to let this go. She's not yours. She's been using you. She's still using you. Let. It. Fucking. Go.

Stassi sighs, interrupting my stream of consciousness. "Families are complicated. I'm sorry, Ro," she reaches for Roisin's hand. "I met Kieran. He was a dick. I'm glad he's dead."

"I am too," Roisin whispers.

Fuck. This.

I stand, running a hand through my hair. "I have to go," I growl. Without another word, I leave the dining room, the women holding onto each other as I storm out.

I shouldn't have agreed to this.

The manor isn't huge, but I head straight for the front door. Choosing to be around Roisin like this was a fucking stupid idea.

I can't stop myself, it seems, from caring about her. I can't stop myself from wanting to help her and protect her.

Which is so fucking stupid, because she's not mine.

She never was.

And even though we're faking it right now...

She never will be.

The garden is cold and dead, and I'm more than happy to add to the general ambiance as I bring my poor attitude outside.

The night is cold. Bitterly so. It feels good against my skin, which is still broiling from the emotions I felt inside.

I'm a fucking wreck.

And I feel so out-of-control, it's fucking killing me.

I take deep breaths, letting the cold, damp air sear into my lungs. My Nonna would have a fit if she could see me out here, sucking in air like I'm a fish out of water when that air is probably more full of moisture than the sea nearby.

I'm finally more in control of my breathing when I'm aware of my phone buzzing in my pocket.

I frown. The phone is the one I keep on me at all times for my family to reach me. It's intensely secure, and only a handful of people on the planet have the access that it gives. Normally I use burner phones, but this one is for family.

And for emergencies only.

Fear flushes through me, and I grab the phone, hesitating as I turn it over to see who it is. My money, of course, is on Dino, who tends to need the most consistent support, but Sal might also...

I pause.

It's not either of my brothers, or my sister, or Luna, my niece who has just recently received her own cell phone and absolutely has the number to my private line.

It's... my brother-in-law.

And former best friend.

Frowning, I pick up the phone. "Elio?"

"Marco," he rumbles, his Italian accent thick enough to make me concerned. It tends to become a little stronger when he's upset or in trouble.

"What? What happened? What's—"

"Nothing. No. Nothing like that," he says quickly.

I pause.

There's an awkward moment where I'm not sure if I should ask him what he wants to say, or if I should just wait.

I wait.

Elio clears his throat. "Ah. Well. How... are you faring?"

He also tends to fuck up and use weird English words when he's nervous. "Fine," I reply curtly.

"I see. Are things well with.. whatever you are doing?"

"Get to the fucking point, Elio," I bark.

He huffs, the sound very European. "Am I not allowed to see how one of my... how someone I know and... find... that I..."

I've never heard Elio be this inarticulate. "Jesus Christ, are you fuckin' choking?" I say.

"I want to see how you are doing, motherfucker!" he practically shouts.

I blink.

"Did you just call me to check in on me, Elio?"

He mutters curses in Italian. "Yes."

Huh. Interesting. "Uh. Okay. Why?"

"What do you mean, why? Why am I supposed to ask how you are? Why am I someone you need to ask why I am checking in on you?"

I cough. "Sorry. Uh. I just didn't... think..."

"I know what you think. And I think it is bullshit. I should be allowed to call in and check on my friend," he snaps.

The word, *friend*, seems to hit me smack in the middle of my chest.

"Are we friends?" I blurt.

Fuck me. I haven't lost control of my mouth this frequently since I was a fucking teenager.

"I would like to be friends," Elio says.

Well.

Elio mutters. Like a sullen, pouting child.

I sigh.

Elio and I were once best friends. We're the same age, and we shared some fun experiences when I was in college and grad school. Elio's father was old-fashioned, and after we graduated high school, Elio returned to Italy to learn to run their business, but we remained friends and would try to get together to party whenever we could. We were young and stupid and jacked up on the kind of hormones that make you feel invincible, and we fucked and partied our way through Europe for long enough that it was cause for some concern. Our families negotiated for him to marry Catarina, my youngest sister, and it changed our friendship, because instead of watching my best friend hook up with women, I was watching my future brother-in-law, and it was a mirror to my own behavior.

And I didn't like what I saw.

Then, Elio and Caterina got engaged, and my parents were murdered.

I assumed Elio to be behind the hit.

And I hated him. For years.

So no, I don't think we're friends.

Or I didn't.

Clearly, Elio notices my silence, because he clears his throat. "Unless you do not wish—"

"We're friends," I interrupt.

Fuck it.

I can be friends with Elio.

Right?

He huffs. "I do not wish to be friends if you do not wish it, Marco. But I..." he pauses.

It's pathetic how interested I am in this pause.

"Occasionally, I find that I require a friend," he says finally.

I think about the situation here. The secrets I'm holding. The secrets I've always held, to keep my family safe.

I've always been okay with it.

Except now?

Those secrets seem heavier than they have ever been.

And most of all, I've held all of these secrets to keep my family safe. To keep my siblings safe. To make them happy.

But I haven't been happy. I haven't been safe.

And I am profoundly and completely fucking alone.

Fuck it, indeed.

"You know what, Elio? Fuck it," I say. "I could use a fucking friend too."

He chuckles. "I take it your endeavors are going well?"

"Fuck no," I bite out.

In the garden, in Liam MacAntyre's family home, within earshot of the woman that's currently tangling my life into knots, I start to talk. I tell Elio about some things. Not everything, of course, because even if we're friends, I don't fucking trust him.

I don't trust anyone.

It feels shitty, to tell him partial truths, but as he hesitates on some things as well, I can tell that he's doing the same thing. Elio's tells might be more obvious than mine, but neither one of us is in a place to give the whole truth.

Yet.

But fuck it feels good to just get some of it out there.

Finally, the words slow, and I heave a sigh.

"My friend," Elio says, the laughter clear in his voice. "I think you have a fucking problem."

"No shit," I mutter.

Roisin is a problem.

And for the first time, I have no fucking solution.

10

ROISIN

The morning brings a hangover and the oppressing reminder of the fact that I'm thirty days away from being locked behind bars, a wanted criminal in my own organization. It's early; the clock on my phone points out that normally, I'd still be asleep at this time. Too fucking early, definitely. The rest of the house probably isn't awake yet, but the champagne still fizzing in my veins clearly had an impact. I get up, brush my teeth and run a comb through my hair, then settle back into the comfortable bed. The light on the walls is the dove-gray particular to the very beginnings of dawn, and I let myself soak it in while trying to sort through the racing thoughts in my head.

The despair hits me like a sucker punch.

No chance of seeing my mom again.

No chance of finding her.

No chance of falling in love or having a family or just fucking going to Ibiza for the weekend, or doing any of the other things that I've toyed with doing with my life after I found my mom.

Jail. Forever.

For a crime I didn't do.

Stassi put me in one of the guest bedrooms, which I'm kind of grateful for. I did have a room here, once, but I have no attachment to it. The guest room is perfect, a soft blend of fabrics with cream tones that work well with the ancient stone walls. It's not even freezing in here, which I attribute to the prolific use of space heaters, and what I suspect might be a sub-floor heater under the luxurious rugs at my feet.

The bed linens are soft. They feel relatively new, and I know that they weren't here when I last left the manor house. Granted, that was a good deal of years ago, but still.

They look nice. Soft. Neutral. Nothing to let anyone know about the fucking vicious past that these walls have witnessed.

I look down, surprised at the feeling of a tear slipping out of my eyes. I scrub my hand against my face, trying to stem the rest of them.

There's nothing to cry about, Ro. You'll figure it out. They won't arrest you. Marco will help...

And then he'll leave.

Again.

A soft knock on my door makes me suck in a breath quickly, tugging the sheets up to wipe away the rest of the tears. "Yes?" I call, annoyed at the thickness in my voice as I try to clear the last of the sadness from it.

"It's me," Marco rumbles.

Fuck.

I went to bed in the guest room last night alone, thinking that it would be less suspicious to try and find Marco and get him settled, but now I realize that I might have made a mistake. Liam is never going to buy that Marco and I sleep in separate rooms.

I just thought that since Marco wasn't with me when I went to bed, it wouldn't make sense for me to send someone to gather him. Normal couples would just wait until one of them wanted to go to bed.

Right?

"Roisin, open the door."

God. Damn. It.

I hate how I respond almost immediately to his commanding voice. My muscles lurch forward, like a puppy, eager to follow his every command.

I'm on my feet before I even know what's happening, and I approach the door so quickly, I pause for a second because I don't want to make it seem like I'm hopping to his every command.

"Roisin—"

I pull the door open. "What?" I hiss.

Marco steps inside, the movement bringing him overwhelmingly close to me. The heat rolling off of his chest, the smell of his skin, momentarily overwhelms me. I step back, just trying to put space between us.

The door clicks softly behind him, closing on hinges that are absolutely new, because when I lived in this house every single hinge squeaked bloody fucking murder when you closed the door.

Which my father liked to punish me for. With his fucking fist.

The reminder of the darkness that haunts this house brings the crushing sorrow back.

Full force.

I spin, so that Marco can't see the tears in the corners of my eyes. "Where were you last night?"

"Garden."

I blink. "All night?"

Marco studies me. "I was talking to Elio," he says after a moment.

Oh.

"Do you... usually talk to Elio all night?" I ask. I know that he doesn't. or at least, he didn't when we were... living together.

It's not being together. It was when I held him in custody in witness protection.

But I don't know how else to describe the relationship we had. We were living together, I was holding him in custody.

But there was more. There was absolutely so much more.

He shrugs. "It's new."

"Okay. Well. Good for you, I think," I mutter. I eye the bed. If I just tug the sheets back, he won't be able to see the tear stains...

I go for it.

Quickly, I tuck myself back in, pulling the covers up around my chin. I look at him, then glance at a chair that Stassi tucked up under the window. "You can sit there."

"I've been out in the cold all night," he growls.

"And you smell like it," I say. It's a cheap shot, I know. But I don't know what I'm going to do if Marco climbs into the bed.

He glowers at me.

Without saying another word, Marco grabs his bag and stomps into the bathroom attached to the guest suite. I hear the shower come on, and I cower under the blankets.

Stop thinking about him naked, Ro. It's not okay. Just focus on your problems. The fact that you are at risk of losing everything. The fact that you...

The door to the bathroom opens and Marco reappears...

Without a shirt on.

I resist the urge to squeak with shock, and instead roll over. I'm fully ready for Marco to get into the chair, but to my shock, the bed dips.

"What are you doing?" I hiss.

"Sleeping."

My jaw works. I can't believe that he just... got into the bed.

"I recommend you do the same."

I huff. "I was sleeping."

"No, you weren't."

The sound is slightly muffled by the blankets, but I snort again. "How do you know?"

"I heard you crying."

I stiffen. "I wasn't."

"You were."

"No, I wasn't."

"I heard you."

"You heard wrong—"

Abruptly, the bed shifts. The covers get pulled down, and within a heartbeat, Marco looms over me, his eyes dark as he stares down.

"You were crying. And I'm not doing a childish back and forth with you, Roisin. I heard you crying. You have every fucking right to be scared. We're here, but it doesn't sound like your brother or your future sister-in-law is in a position to figure out what happened, or why you're being blamed. Someone in your brother's organization is fucking selling you out, and Liam is going to have to trust both of us in order to figure out who the fuck it is. Hell, it could be him," he grunts.

I look away.

"It's not looking good. But sitting here and arguing with me isn't going to fucking help," Marco mutters.

I don't answer.

He's right. The thought that Liam might be the one who sold me out has crossed my mind, but considering that I'd be able to tell Interpol exactly how fucked he is as a business leader, and where I'd be able to sell his secrets to the highest bidder.

It's not love or commitment, sure, but at least I know that I could hurt him just as badly as he hurts me.

Unless, of course, there's more.

Marco seems to understand, and moves off of me. I breathe, sucking in air that seems oddly cold without his heat to warm it.

"We need to figure out who the fuck did this to you, Roisin. We need to figure it out, fast, because you don't have time to argue with me. For better or worse, I'm here with you. I'm here to fucking figure this shit out."

"And then you'll leave when it's done," I whisper.

It's too vulnerable. Too fragile. The question sits in the air like a glass suspended mid-drop, waiting to hit the ground and explode.

Marco breathes.

"Yes. When it's done, I'll be gone. We'll be connected through Liam, but I have my own family to look after."

I roll over.

The words hit me, somewhere that fucking hurts. I don't want him to see me cry. I don't want him to hear me.

But the fact that he will be gone, after this?

It's the icing on the fucking cake.

Eventually, I suppose I fell asleep, because when I awaken, the light has changed from the soft gray of early morning to the muted, rainy gray of the wintery Irish morning. I sit up, blinking, and notice the lack of male presence next to me.

He's gone.

But, he hasn't left.

I think.

I shower quickly, opting for a comfortable, if luxurious, outfit. Expensive jeans and a cloud-soft cashmere sweater. I do my best to wrangle my hair into a composed state, choosing to keep it back and off of my face, before I head out into the manor.

I have no idea what to do right now.

Marco is, unfortunately, right. I need to start working Liam and Stassi over for information about who might have come up with the plan to frame me in the organization, but I don't know how to do that.

Liam is my brother. For better or worse, I would rather just ask him outright.

And Stassi is... Stassi.

She is the unknown, though. So I do probably need to start there.

Sighing, I head into the kitchen, in search of my future sister-in-law.

Stassi, poised and perfect as always, is sitting in the kitchen. I note with some satisfaction that her outfit echoes mine; dark, well fitting jeans, and a black sweater that also looks quite soft.

Stassi, however, looks like a literal model, and I give her sleek blonde hair an envious glance before sliding in next to her.

"Morning," I say, reaching for the pastries displayed on the table in front of her.

"Oh my god. I'm so happy you're awake!" Stassi beams. "Okay so, I'm thinking today that we need to go into town and run some errands."

My fingers freeze on the croissants. "What for?"

"Well, I need to confirm some things with the florist, and I think that someone in town has a really cute little stationery shop that I'm thinking of using for the invitations."

"Invitations?"

Stassi nods. "Liam agreed that we need to make sure people buy into what we're doing. So. Invitations, flowers, the whole nine yards. My mom will never believe that we're getting married unless I really sell her on it, you know?"

Slowly, I pull my hand back. "You've said this a couple of times, Stassi. Are you in love with my brother?"

She rolls her eyes. "God, no."

I blink.

Stassi sighs. "I mean, I'm not trying to say he's like a bad guy or anything like that, you know? He seems fine, comparatively. But like, I owed Gia Rossi this huge favor, and there was a lot at stake with a marriage contract that she's supposed to have with one of your brothers—"

"One of them?" I say sharply.

Stassi nods. "Well, technically I guess it was Caterina, which set off like a whole chain of events a while ago. But then Gia got kidnapped by Liam, who was trying to make an alliance with the Rossi crew because like, they're pretty darn powerful, and Kieran was many things but a good leader wasn't one of them, you know?"

I narrow my eyes. Stassi is either the best actress in the entire world, or she actually fucking trusts me with this.

"Anyway," she continues, sipping her latte. "Gia and Sal had this whole problem, and Liam needed someone to marry, and I said okay here I am."

"So, you don't love him?"

She shrugs. "Why would I fall in love with my husband? That seems like a sure-fire way to get a broken heart."

I snort. "I don't know what to do with that."

"Oh, come on. Tell me a single person you know who fell in love with their husband and actually stayed that way. Especially in our world, men don't play by the rules," she says.

I glance at Stassi. Her voice is so much harder now, the bubbly blonde receding. "I think that Marco's siblings seem to be pretty happy."

"There's still time for all of that to fall apart," she chirps cheerily.

Something about this beautiful, fun person talking about the prevalence of heartbreak feels kind of... wrong. "Stassi, you know that any man would be falling over their fucking feet to have you, right? Men literally worship the ground you walk on."

She looks away. "Yeah, but there's a big difference in how men treat women like that and how they treat a partner."

"Okay. You're going to have to say more about that."

Stassi looks at me. "Men like pretty things. They like to look at them, take them out and play with them, and then put them back on the shelf. They don't want me, Ro. They want to look at me and parade me around, but then I'll go back on the shelf with everyone else," she whispers. "And when something else pretty catches their eye? I'll be locked away. Forever."

Jesus Christ. "Stassi..."

"My mom taught me that. She was Ivan Novikov's pretty thing. And she was fine with that. She knew how to get what she needed and then just get out. My mom was fine with the shelf. I'm not," she whispers.

I search her face. "And Liam?"

She winks. "I don't want him. He doesn't want me. It's perfect."

There is absolutely no way that my brother doesn't want Anastasia Novikov. It's fucking insane to think that he doesn't. "There's no way that's true."

"Oh, I wouldn't be doing this if it wasn't. So," she says, giving me that bright smile. "Flowers?"

Slowly, I nod.

"I'll get my coat."

Stassi glides through my brother's staff like she's meant to be here. She knows them, already. She's asked about four babies and has offered condolences to one grandmother by the time we pull into the village, which is by no means as elevated as the shopping that Marco and I did in Dublin. But, I will say as we walk around, Doolin appears to have become at least a little more modern since I was here last year.

The shops, at least, have figured out that high-end tourists are their target market.

Stassi drags me to not one, but two florists, and by the time we're headed for the stationery shop, I can't believe the fact that she's already signed contracts with both.

"How do you do that?" I ask.

She smiles. "Do what?"

"Every person you meet isn't a stranger, instantly. You somehow not only signed that contract, but got an invite to come over for dinner tomorrow."

"Oh my god, I know!" she beams. "Mrs. Murtagh was just the cutest old lady, there's no way that I'm going to say no!"

I laugh. "See? That's what I'm talking about. You don't have a single bad thing to say about them. Everyone, even strangers, love you. Like, instantly."

She shrugs. "I guess it's my mom. She was raised by people who were Hollywood stars for the past... well, since movies started coming out. If she knows how to do anything, she knows how to socialize, because she and her family basically invented it."

"Well that's all well and good," I say, following her into the stationery shop. "But you somehow find something to like about everyone you meet."

"Why wouldn't I?" Stassi beams. "Everyone has something they bring to the world. It's just a matter of seeing it."

Good lord.

For a moment, I'm insanely jealous of Stassi. How in the world she and I both managed to be raised by men in the mafia, with mothers adjacent to it, and we turned out so... different, is beyond me.

I don't see the good in everyone I meet.

Because I'm too busy trying to figure out the ways that they could hurt me, so that I can hurt them first.

Stassi waves at me. "Over here! Look, these are the invites that I was telling you—"

The door to the shop tinkles, and a chill of fear instantly skates down my spine.

Something isn't fucking right.

My hand instinctively goes to my hip, where my Interpol-issued gun would usually be, but I feel nothing except soft cashmere instead.

Fuck.

Stassi is chatting, looking at paper samples. I don't want to turn to confront whoever just walked into the shop, but the little room is so small, I don't have any other way to look and see them.

So, slowly, I turn.

I lock eyes with someone that makes my heart skip a beat.

Andrei Moretti.

He's a famed assassin. Most recently, he's been in Brazil, and he's got a list of crimes so long they span the Atlantic.

And he's here.

In a fucking paper shop in Ireland.

Behind us.

There's absolutely no way that he's here for anything except something bad. Moretti has been nicknamed the Grim Reaper, and some other names that are rolling through my mind.

Angel of Death.

Assassin's assassin.

We need to get the fuck out of here.

I look over at Stassi, trying to catch her eye.

She's entirely focused on paper samples.

"...I really think that at such short notice, we should go with something more casual, don't you think?"

"Yes," I respond, aware of Moretti coming closer. The shop is tiny. He's practically breathing down our necks. If he hasn't shot either of us yet, he's probably here on capture orders.

Which means a sedative.

Which means we need to get the fuck out of here.

In my pocket, my fingers reach for my phone. If I can call Marco...

"And what do you think for the envelopes? Cream or eggshell?" Stassi points.

"Stassi, I don't feel well," I whisper in her ear.

She blinks at me. "What?"

"I need to leave. Right now."

"Um, okay, but..."

I tug on her hand. "Please, it's the... it's my cramps," I add.

If Moretti is listening, I'm hopeful that the mention of something feminine will put him off. You'd be surprised at how often men, even ones with killer intent, hesitate when it comes to a period.

Stassi frowns. "Okay, but..."

"Now," I tug on her hand.

I can't linger. I know she's going to want to talk to the shop owner, who I really hope isn't going to be a casualty of Moretti too. I drag Stassi, who is trying to wave down the shop keep, out the door.

When we get outside, she tugs her hand back. "What the heck, Ro? You feel that bad? I swear, that was so rude—"

"Andrei Moretti walked into the shop behind us," I whisper.

Stassi's blue eyes widen, then her face goes pale. "What?"

It's good to know, I guess, that she finally understands the severity of the situation. "We need to fucking go," I whisper.

"What? How on earth would he... I thought he was in Brazil? I thought he died in that landslide?"

"Nope," I shake my head, dragging my phone out to call for our driver. "He was right fucking here, in the shop with us."

"Let me call for the driver..."

A booming noise, followed by searing heat, cuts her off.

Instinctively, I grab Stassi. She's a head or so taller than I am, but I'm stronger, and I wrestle her to the ground. The sound of the explosion echoes around the picturesque seaside village, and I hear screaming from the direction of where we parked.

Stassi's eyes widen. "Roisin. Do you think..."

"Call Liam," I hiss. "Now."

My fingers are already pulling up Marco's number. I dial it, my fingers flying across the screen.

He picks up on the first ring. "Roisin, what—"

"Andrei Moretti is in town. The car blew up. Come get us," I hiss.

Then, I shut the phone off, and grab Stassi's hand.

I tug her toward the explosion.

"Where are we going? Don't go this way, we need..."

"We need to hide. Moretti probably set the bomb to start a distraction so he could take you or me," I murmur.

Stassi follows. "So why are we going to the explosion?"

"Because that's where a crowd will be. We're harder to kidnap in a crowd," I mutter.

Already, people are running out of their homes and businesses, and the screaming gets louder as we approach the explosion.

My heart sinks.

The people of Doolin are peaceful. They live in a sleepy seaside town.

God, I hope no one died.

Praying, we move closer. I want to keep looking back for

Moretti, but I don't want him to know that I'm watching for him.

"Look behind us," I whisper to Stassi. "Do you see Moretti?"

"I don't know what he looks like…"

"Dark and fucking mean," I hiss.

She turns her head. "I don't think so."

"Good. Stay with me. Don't let go of my hand. He wants one of us, and I don't know who. He probably has a sedative, so keep a distance from other people so he can't stick you."

Stassi breathes.

The site of the explosion finally comes into view. My chest sags with relief. Our driver, David, is standing, looking shaken, leaning on the seawall. The SUV is on fire, but there's no obvious bodies.

Good.

"Don't go to him. Stick near the road, Marco will be here any second," I whisper.

Stassi and I stand back, out of the way, where we can easily leave. When the Jaguar pulls up that Marco bought the other day, I grab her.

"Let's go."

Marco doesn't even stop. I open the door and shove Stassi in, then climb in. He peels out while the car burns in the background, and as soon as I shut the door again I look out.

There, standing next to the seawall, is Andrei Moretti.

And he's staring at us as we drive away.

11

MARCO

The engine revs as I slam my foot on the accelerator. I speed along the road back to Aughris House, my hands practically strangling the steering wheel as I go.

When Roisin called, I wasn't doing anything important. Just following Liam around, trying to get a handle on what he spends his day doing. I want him to trust me, but I don't have time to get him to do so.

Instead, I decided early this morning after I left Roisin sleeping in the bed to resort to old-fashioned spy work to try and figure out what the fuck is going on.

Liam, of course, is the prime suspect for all the fucking bullshit that Roisin has walked into. He's her brother, sure, but as we know from Kieran, being a sibling in this fucking family means exactly fuck all.

Following Liam required stealth, and I was perfectly happy to do it...

Until my cell rang.

Opening it, I found Roisin's number, and I took the call, ducking into a different room so Liam didn't hear me.

When she spoke, I heard the cool, detached tone of an Interpol agent.

Which meant that something was fucking bad.

And then, when she said Moretti's name, coupled with an explosion?

I knew it was really fucking bad.

I didn't even bother trying to catch Liam up. I jumped into the Jag and headed to town, desperate to find Roisin.

To make sure that she was okay.

Now, she and Stassi are sitting in the back seat. Stassi looks rattled, her blonde hair disheveled, her face pale.

Roisin looks…

Well.

Roisin looks like she's calculating revenge.

A rush of pride swells in my chest. *That's my fucking girl.*

She's not your girl, dickwad.

"What happened?" I snarl.

Roisin looks at Stassi. "Should we wait for Liam?"

"Tell me. Right the fuck now."

The manor house is practically in view. I know that I should wait for Liam but…

I don't give a fuck.

"We went shopping. Stassi wanted to run some errands for the wedding , and I agreed to go with her. We made it through two shops just fine, but by the time we got to the third Moretti found us. He didn't shoot on site so I'm assuming he was trying to kidnap one of us, maybe both. Probably had a sedative in his pocket but was trying to avoid attention, which makes me think that it was sanctioned or something. Either way, the explosion was a clear distraction, and he wanted us."

My hands tighten on the steering wheel.

I live in a world of bad men. I know, deeply, the awful things that people can do to each other, and I know that I've done them in order to preserve my own family. There's nothing that I wouldn't do to keep them safe, and I'd sell my fucking soul to do it.

But Andrei Moretti is a different type of evil.

I'm anchored to my family. He has no anchor. He's willing to turn on anyone and everyone, and sells his ability to sin to the highest bidder, regardless of whether or not he believes in the cause. There's nothing that money won't buy with him, and there's no task that he won't do.

There's also no amount of pain that he won't cause.

Recently, he was employed by Benicio Souza, the cartel leader who happens to be my sister-in-law Marisol's father. Benicio died in an accident, but Moretti was kind of obsessed with Marisol, if their account is right.

And now, he seems to be obsessed with Roisin.

Or Stassi.

Something, however, makes me think that whoever hired Moretti is also the one who tried to frame Roisin.

And whoever it is, they're someone with deep fucking pockets.

We pull into the drive and Liam is standing there, his face marked with fury. When Roisin opens the door, he immediately barks, "What the fuck? Why did I just get a call from David saying that the fucking car exploded?"

"Because the car exploded," Roisin says in her same even tone.

Liam's face contorts. "The *fucking car exploded*," he yells, "and not a fuckin' one of you thought to call me! What the—"

"Yell like that again and see what happens," Stassi interrupts.

We all turn to look at her.

Because that voice?

It's cold as ice.

Liam immediately stops. His face is bright red and his eyes are wild, but he's looking at Stassi with something I recognize.

Because it's exactly how I felt when Roisin called me.

"Can someone please, for the love of God, tell me what is going on?" Liam says slowly.

We all turn to look at Roisin, who raises an eyebrow at me. "Told you we should have waited for Liam."

I don't care.

I listen to Roisin relate the story again, her detached tone completely impassive as she goes through the details. She's a wonderful police officer, certainly.

But I itch to get more out of her than just this.

The detachment makes me uncomfortable. When I think of Roisin, of all the things she told me and all the things I've recently learned, this is a woman who has been through a lot of suffering in her life.

And hearing her voice, it's clear to me that the way she's learned to handle it is to just... not feel anything.

It bothers me. It makes me want to irritate her, to get her angry.

To make her feel *something*, so that this strange, flat person isn't in front of me anymore.

Roisin finishes, taking a deep breath. She looks at her brother, folding her arms.

"Any idea why the most feared assassin in the world might be coming for your fiancé and your sister?"

"Or my sister," he mutters.

Roisin's eyebrows raise.

Liam shrugs. "We don't know that he was coming for both of you. It could have been either one. So before we jump to conclusions, I think it's important to say that it could have been either one of you, or both. Three options."

"Fine," Roisin spits. "Any reason that someone would be coming for your fiancé *or* your sister, *or* both of them?"

Liam's nostrils flare, and he shoots me a meaningful glare.

Fuck you, man.

"If you think that you're going to try and fucking hide something from me like this, when Roisin was one of the targets, then you're fucking delusional," I growl.

His eyes narrow. "And what's it to you then? You've said many times your only loyalty is to your family. So what's Roisin to you? Not family," he snarls.

I step forward, until the space between Liam and I is compressed. We're about evenly matched in height, and I stare into his fucking eyes like I'm about to take down a bear.

"Roisin is *mine*," I snarl.

The vehemence rocks me. It's the truth, and while I've been trying to deny it, I can't anymore.

Roisin is mine.

And I'll fucking deal with what that means at another time.

But today?

I'll burn the world down for her.

12

ROISIN

I have to do something, or Marco and Liam are going to fight.

Stepping forward, I grab Marco's wrist. "Look, it happened. We don't know why. I'm fucking tired and I want to take a shower and then we can figure out whether it was Stassi or me, okay?"

Marco doesn't move from looking at Liam. "I'm here to fucking help," he grunts. "If you don't want that, that's your fucking problem. Not mine."

Lord save me from fucking idiotic men. "I can save myself. I just need to have a gun next time and we'll be good. And Stassi was there too, Liam. Don't you want to check in on your fiancé?"

Liam's eyes dart to her, noticing her pale face and shaken expression for the first time. It's like a switch flips in his mind, and his face flushes red. He doesn't say anything to Marco or me, his eyes drifting back over to Stassi, who looks at him with the type of hurt that makes me question a whole lot about what she said to me earlier.

You might not want to care about your husband, Stassi, but I think you care a whole lot whether he cares about you.

"Let's go," Marco says, wrapping his fingers around my wrist.

I follow him.

We don't speak. Once we're inside the house, we go straight to the guest room. I leave Marco standing there, and I close the door behind myself as I enter the little bathroom.

I need to clean off the day.

When I was growing up, the one place my brother and my dad wouldn't bother me was the bathroom. I don't know if it was just their one thing that they wouldn't do, or if it was common decency, or what, but I would turn the shower on and immediately have some time to myself.

So now, whenever I'm stressed or anxious, I'm immediately going to take a shower.

Like right now.

I strip the clothes off, trying not to think about the fact that I very well could have died out there. Instead, I focus on the process. Jeans off. Sweater off. Water on.

I'm in the shower, trying to shake the feeling of being hunted by the world's worst assassin, when I hear the door click open.

For a second I tense, until I hear Marco say softly, "It's me."

"I'm in the shower," I snap.

"I know. I'm not... I just want to talk."

"About what?"

He hesitates for a second, and all I can hear is the sound of running water.

"About what happened."

I sigh, shutting the water off. I stick my arm out of the curtain. "Hand me a towel."

A fluffy, thick towel appears in my hand.

I wrap it around myself, not bothering to dry my hair, and I step out.

Marco blinks. For a second, I relish the sensation of his eyes tracing the curve of my neck.

The darkness in his gaze.

Then, I remember.

He's leaving.

Sighing, I turn. "What do you want to talk about?"

I'm not watching him. It's the only reason that I don't see what comes next.

It all happens so fast.

His hand grabs my arm and turns me. I look up, ready to tell him off, but I never get the chance.

His lips crash over mine.

This isn't just a kiss.

It's a revelation.

I might not be insanely experienced when it comes to men, but I can tell right away that this kiss?

It's something different.

I moan, my fingers rising to skate through Marco's hair as I tip my head back. He devours me, one hand curling around the back of my neck in a gesture that's possessive enough to make me shudder, and the other splayed on my jaw, forcing me into a position that is completely at his mercy.

This is nothing like our last kiss.

Heat scorches my body, racing over every scrap of my skin. I gasp as Marco's mouth descends to my neck, lighting me up with kiss after kiss that seems to electrify every single nerve in my body.

I tuck him closer, running my nails down his neck. My other hand creeps up to where the towel is wrapped around my shoulders. I should just drop it...

Abruptly, Marco steps back.

His eyes are so dark they look like pools of ink. His lips, which have always been unfairly pretty for a man, are parted, and his hair is in disarray.

He looks like I feel.

Frazzled. Unsteady.

Devastated by that kiss.

Peering down at me, he gives a sharp nod.

"Finally."

I blink. "Finally what?"

"Finally, the fucking brick wall is gone."

Either my brain is completely toast, or he's making no sense. "Huh?"

"You," Marco breathes. "You were... different."

"When?"

"Just now. When we were in the car."

"In the..." my voice trails off. I must look terribly confused, because Marco's lips thin into a frustrated line.

"You weren't you, Roisin. It was like talking to someone who had completely just... you were gone," he growls.

I have absolutely no idea what he's saying. Frustration makes his jaw clench, and he spins. "Never fucking mind," he mutters.

The bathroom door slams behind him.

Leaving me alone.

Naked.

And still shaking from that kiss.

When I fully compose myself, I'm ready to give Marco a piece of my fucking mind.

He doesn't get to just... *do* that.

Walk into the bathroom, kiss me like the world's ending, and then... blame me for something that's utterly and completely illogical.

You weren't you.

I was *me*.

Just... the version of me that's a little more guarded. I guess.

As I should be, though.

I huff, my thoughts swirling as I rip open the door to my room and stomp down the hallway. I'm not sure why he thinks that I would just be completely unphased after *that*.

Andrei Moretti is not exactly someone that you just... walk away from.

Now that he's involved, everything feels more complicated. Because while it's possible that Moretti is after Anastasia, I think it's significantly more likely that the people who are trying to frame me for murder and the people who hired Moretti are, in fact, the same people.

Which would be very, very bad.

I don't have time for this.

If I have to figure out who is framing me, then I can't also spend time trying to run from Moretti. I need to be able to hide here with Stassi and Liam, using Marco as my cover story, without also worrying about Andrei Moretti trying to find me.

My first instinct, honestly, is to run.

It's the only way I can be guaranteed that I won't die.

My survival instincts are more than just a little triggered, at the moment.

They're going haywire.

One thing I definitely, absolutely, completely do not need is Marco bringing up... anything.

Or kissing me.

Or kissing me like he just kissed me, like the world was on fire.

Like I was precious to him.

Like I mattered to him.

It put me right back to that night in the cozy little cabin near the sea. When we were pretending to be a couple. When we spent every day living as though our real selves didn't exist.

But that's the problem, isn't it?

Our real selves do exist. I'm Roisin MacAntyre. He's Marco DeLuca.

The little bubble of happiness that we had out there? It wasn't real. It wasn't even close to real.

And when it became real, everything between us broke wide open.

Marco, unfortunately, is nowhere to be found.

Instead, I find Liam and Stassi, sitting together in the kitchen. Stassi looks furious, and Liam looks…

Well, also furious, but in an entirely different way.

I plop down into one of the dining room chairs. "Hi," I mutter.

Stassi sucks in a huge breath, like she's trying as hard as she can to move the conversation out of the mud they've stuck it in. "Feeling better?"

"A little," I say.

I'm not feeling any better. Especially because, by my estimation, things went from bad to worse when Marco and I kissed.

Even if it was the most delicious kiss you've ever experienced…

I give myself a little shake. "Where's Marco?"

"Taking a call in the garden," Liam says. His eyes turn to me, looking a little too bright. "Thought he told you that?"

Oops.

Yes, someone's romantic partner would, potentially, know when they were taking a call.

Instead of letting Liam dig further into my slip-up, I throw my shoulders back and give him a look. "And you're just going to let him do that without spying on him?"

"Do I need to spy on your boyfriend, little sister?," Liam retorts.

Damn.

"The garden's bugged anyway," Stassi waves a hand. "And I'm sure Marco knows that."

He probably does.

I sigh. This type of constant cat-and-mouse is exhausting. Just one of a million reasons that I don't like being around men like the men in my family.

Like Marco.

You can never really relax. You have to constantly stay vigilant.

And no one is ever, *ever,* safe.

"So. Are we going to talk about why Andrei Moretti is after one of the two of you, then?" Liam's eyebrows raise.

I open my mouth, some kind of lie brewing on my tongue, but Stassi beats me to it. "It's probably me," she says with a little bit of a laugh.

The somewhat meaningful glance she throws my way makes me feel like there's more for her and I to discuss later.

Liam tucks his arms across his chest, leaning back in his chair. "Why?"

"Well, I'm like a Russian mafia princess, right? Who wouldn't be after me?"

The deliberate use of the vapid-sounding voice won't throw Liam off. His gaze sharpens on her. "That's it, is it?"

"Well yeah," Stassi tosses her hair over her shoulder. "I can think of like, at least ten different guys who would want to marry me."

"Can you now?" Liam practically purrs.

Oh. Interesting.

This version of Liam is a little more dangerous, perhaps, and while I'm not concerned for anyone's safety, I am curious how my future sister-in-law is going to handle this.

Intrigued, I straighten in my chair.

"Obviously. I'm a catch, Liam."

This is getting dangerously close to flirting.

But Anastasia Novikov has made it very, very clear that she's not going to be flirting with my brother anytime soon.

Unless, of course, it suits some other purpose of hers.

Liam, bless his soul, hasn't figured out a damn thing yet. "But who is trying to catch you, Anastasia," he growls. "They can't do a fuckin' thing, because you're going to be my wife. Mine."

Ohhhhhh boy.

There it is.

I stand. "Well. I'm off to find Marco, then."

"Ro—"

"You two enjoy this," I wave a hand.

I leave my brother and his fiancé, staring at each other, and I give a small laugh as I walk away.

Stassi and Liam have something going on. Whatever it is, it's theirs to figure out. But from the sound of the possession in his voice? My brother's falling hard.

For a woman who, under no circumstances, wants to love her husband.

Marco's in the barn.

I went to the garden first, naturally, but he wasn't there. Since I didn't think that Marco had just up and left, I reasoned that he was somewhere. Initially, I had just decided I would simply hear from him later, and walked away.

But I wanted to go to the barn.

Riding, when I was little, was something my mother had made me do. In her head, proper Irish girls, whether they be raised in the city or the country, needed to be able to ride a horse. My father and Kieran hadn't thought I was a capable rider, so I hadn't done much riding during that time in my life, but I still loved to be around horses.

And the barn, apparently, is where Marco decided to end up as well.

I freeze in the door when I first walk in. He's petting one of the horses, a tall hunter with a lovely chestnut coat and a blaze on its forehead. Marco's lips are curled into a smile, and while

I can't hear his words, the soothing cadence of them feels like I'm watching an entirely different Marco.

One that I might have called mine...

Once.

"I didn't know you liked horses," I say, choosing to announce my presence.

To both of their credit, neither the horse nor Marco startles. Marco produces a treat from his pocket, and the horse nibbles at it enthusiastically.

Stepping inside the barn, I let the horse sniff my fingers. The velvet of its lips tickles my palms, and when it gives me a friendly little nibble as well, I laugh.

"Elio's family had horses. I grew up riding them."

"Elio's family?" I raise my eyebrows.

Marco nods. "We were close, as kids. Each of us being the heir to our respective families gave a unique perspective on things, and it's hard to find people who occupy a similar space."

"Your siblings?"

Shaking his head, Marco puts his hands in his pockets. "They're part of why it's a unique space."

"What do you mean?"

He sighs. "It's hard to explain. And I think that Liam might understand, somewhat."

"I'm a slight smarter than my brother, you know," I say dryly.

"Of that I have no doubt."

Marco's quiet for a moment. I look at the horse, leaning forward to pet its forehead.

"You feel responsible for them," I say, guessing at the kind of turmoil he's hinting at.

"I am responsible for them."

"Even now? They're grown, with families and children of their own to look after," I murmur. Part of it is reality, but part of it is my own experience.

I don't want Liam looking after me forever, after all.

In fact, I don't want him looking after me in the slightest.

"In this world, I will always be responsible for them," he says softly.

Something in his voice feels... hard.

"But you don't want that," I say, again, reading between the lines of his words. "You don't want to be responsible for them. Not anymore."

Marco is silent.

I sigh, dropping my hand from the horse. "If it helps, I'd rather no one be responsible for me."

"Yeah?" he sounds amused.

I nod, emphatically. "It's a kind of torture, I think."

"How so?"

"Because, it's infantilizing. How am I supposed to be my own person, to exist as myself, if I'm constantly being told that someone else is responsible for me? Liam isn't in charge of my decisions. He's alright. Not a bad one, I suppose. But Kieran..." my voice trails off.

Kieran was anything but *alright*.

"Being at the whims of a sociopath was a specific kind of misery, Marco. I don't want people to be responsible for me. I am responsible for myself, and that's the way it's going to be," I say.

Marco snorts. "Well, good luck with that."

"What does that mean?"

He leans against one of the wooden stalls. "I mean good luck with that. Since you needed me to pretend to date you, so that we could get back and spy on your brother."

"I—" I open my mouth to protest, but it snaps shut.

Marco's face tightens. "That's what I thought."

"Marco—"

The air around us, so calm and peaceful, suddenly shatters.

Gunshots.

The noise is unmistakable, and when you've grown up the way I have, you'll never mistake anything for a gunshot. The noise is burned into my very cells.

I hit the ground, Marco next to me.

My first thought is for Stassi and Liam. I want to get back to them, to make sure they're okay.

But when the gunshots continue to rattle around us, I know that's not an option. Liam and Stassi will have to get out of this on their own.

Because with this many agents firing around us, we need to get out of here with our own lives before we lose them.

The horse, who apparently has been trained enough to make him into a statue, munches his hay, ears pricked forward.

I look at Marco. His face is scrunched in calculation. "Do we..." I start.

The gunshots continue. They don't sound like they're getting closer, but they're joined by machine guns, which I assume come from my brother's security. Heart in my chest, I look over at Marco, my eyes wild.

He looks at me.

Up at the horse.

Then back at me.

"You can ride?" he says.

I nod.

"Move. Fast."

We don't use tack.

There's a gray mare in the stall next to the chestnut that I swing up onto. She's unhappy about it for a second, and her ears flick back, but she appears to be just as well trained as the chestnut. Neither one is particularly bothered by the sound of gunshots, which I count as a blessing, and wonder what on earth my brother might have trained them for.

Marco opens the door to the barn, the one that faces away from the house, and on the horses' backs, we gallop out down the path.

Without reins or a saddle, I'm clutching my mare's mane, my heart beating a tattoo in my chest as we race away. There's shouting, which I assume means that whoever it is that's shooting at the manor has noticed that Marco and I are escaping.

Marco swerves, looking back at me. "Follow me," he says, his voice a low rumble that barely meets my ears.

"Where are we going?"

Marco gives me a look. "Do you trust me, Roisin?"

It's a statement that makes my eyes snap to his.

The horses' hooves thunder down the trail. The wind whips through my hair.

I look at Marco, and I utter one word.

"Yes."

13

MARCO

I HAVE TO KEEP HER SAFE.

With the horse's sides heaving between my legs, and my nerves buzzing with adrenaline, the thought keeps presenting itself over and over again.

I don't give a fuck about Liam right now. I feel a little bad about Stassi, because she's a pretty cool person and I know my sister and Gia both like her a lot, but I needed to get Roisin out of there, and I needed to do it fast.

Abandoning them was the only option.

Racing away from the manor house, I keep Roisin and her horse in my sights at all times. I have no other thoughts in my head, other than one.

I have to keep her safe.

It's extremely goddamn frustrating.

I should leave her there. Liam's business, her business, is

clearly not my business. I should take the opportunity to escape, and run back to my family. Where I belong.

Except I don't fucking belong there.

I don't belong anywhere.

But I absolutely can't let her stay here when I know that she's being fucking hunted.

My mind races as we speed toward the coast.

If we can make it to Donegal, I have a way for us to get the hell out of here.

Roisin isn't going to like it. But hitting the ocean is the only option. Once we get to the coast, if I can find a boat, we can get the fuck off of this island.

And a head start on whoever is hunting her like this.

I know she has questions. Fuck. I have them too.

But we can't answer shit if we're being hunted...

If she's being hunted.

There it is again. I could walk away. Any time.

But Roisin can't.

The horses run, and I direct the chestnut gelding to a path through what looks like some kind of nature preserve. While I normally don't give a shit about nature, I'm grateful now.

The trees provide some cover.

Cover that we desperately need.

The village is probably a half-mile away. If we continue on horseback, we're more likely to be noticed, so I wrap my hands around the horse's neck, murmuring slightly and pulling back.

Well-trained creature that he is, he slows, and the gray mare that Roisin is riding slows too.

The horses pant, their nostrils flaring. I slide off of the chestnut's back, then move to Roisin.

Surprisingly, she lets me wrap my hands around her waist, and I pull her gently off of the beast.

Her face is flushed and her hair is wild. I'm sure it's all tangled, and she's going to need something to tame it with.

I make a note to find something in town.

"Why are we here?" she asks.

My question from earlier surfaces again. *Do you trust me?*

I look at the harbor. "We need a boat."

"A boat? Where—"

"I can get us out of here."

She looks at me, her eyes pinched together with worry. "Liam and Stassi..."

"I can't do anything right now," I say softly.

She looks backwards. "We should go back."

"We can't."

"We should, Marco."

I have to keep her safe.

"All we can do is keep moving forward, Roisin."

"What if they're dead?"

The question is flat. I can't decide if she's already accepted that they might be dead, or if she's hopeful that they haven't.

Roisin is too much of a realist to be hopeful that they aren't dead, I decide.

"They might be."

The statement makes her wince, and I kick myself for not being sensitive enough.

"I'll tell Elio. He and Gia will be able to get a ground force here quickly," I say. I whip out my phone and text Elio that Stassi is in danger, and that he needs to mobilize someone from Italy quickly.

When he confirms, I look back at Roisin.

"They didn't come for Stassi," she murmurs.

It's a confirmation. "They didn't," I murmur.

Roisin's eyes fill with tears.

My heart feels like it crumples as I look at her. She wraps her arms around herself, looking at me through the tears.

"Why is this happening to me?"

"I don't know," I say, my voice a low growl. "But we're going to find out."

The boat from Donegal is small. It stinks, like fish and ocean and the iron-sharp tang of seaweed left to rot in the sun.

Worst of all, though, Roisin has cut herself off from me entirely.

She's wrapped up at the bow of the boat, a fishy blanket around her shoulders. The captain provided it after taking one look at her face. I explained that we were Americans interested in an authentic tour of my homeland, making my face as blankly American as possible.

Given the amount of Americans who come by the dozens to tour the places that their ancestors left, it's not uncommon. I certainly know that Elio and I got away with things in Italy while pretending to be on some kind of homecoming trip.

Elio, of course, is Italian. And I'm Italian enough that it never felt right to say I was discovering Italy… I had always known it.

The boat captain rolled his eyes but agreed to take us on his route, which would stop at another village. My vision from there was to grab a car, steal it if necessary, and then continue on to a larger port. Or even a fucking airport.

I don't think I can get the passports in time, however…

"Your woman. She's gonna catch a cold up there," the captain says behind my shoulder.

It takes years of careful steeling of my nerves to not tell him, aggressively, that she's not my woman.

"She's tougher than you think," I murmur.

"Still. Someone's going to get cold between the two of ye, if you don't have a bed to sleep in for a while. If you need to mend something with her, son, you might as well do it," he murmurs.

God save me from nosy old men.

Still, I have a part to play. I drift up to the bow with Roisin.

"The captain says I need to make sure you aren't mad at me, so I can leave the doghouse," I murmur.

I'm not sure why I'm hoping that the idea of our stupid lie will get a smile out of her. But I am hoping that.

Somehow.

Roisin sighs. "Sure. Well. You've done it. Made up."

"Roisin…"

"What, Marco. Do you want me to say *good job*? Do you want me to say that I'm happy to be here right now, or that everything seems freaking great? It doesn't. I'm a lot of things but I'm not a liar, and right now I'm terrified that my brother is dead and that his very amazing fiancé who never deserved any of this is dead too. I'm worried that I'm going to go to jail for a very long time, for a murder that I didn't cause. So tell me, Marco," she snaps at me. "What the hell do you want from me?"

"I want you…" my voice trails off.

I don't want her to be so defeated.

I don't want her to worry about Liam and Stassi.

I wish I could just… fix all this for her.

Fuck.

This is what I do. I fix things. I do it for my family all the time.

So why the fuck can't I do it for Roisin, somehow?

Roisin's eyes search mine. She gives me just another moment before turning with a sharp nod.

"That's what I thought."

I don't say anything. I stand there, so the captain doesn't question my abilities as a partner and turn us in.

But my mind churns, faster and more quickly than the Irish sea.

As the boat pulls in to the village, my phone beeps. I'm not sure if it's because we finally have a signal or if Elio has only just now gotten information, but I quickly open it.

Elio: Stassi and the fucking Irishman are fine.

There's a relief.

Me: Who organized the hit?

Elio: Why is Andrei Moretti chasing you?

Ah.

Me: Tell you later.

Elio: Friends don't tell friends that.

Me: Yes they do.

Elio: Fuck you. I swear to fucking god, if Moretti comes near my family...

Me: He's in Europe. I'm in Europe. I'll make sure he stays here.

Elio: Use one of the central safe houses.

Now there's an idea.

Me: Thanks.

I snap the phone shut right as we pull up along the dock. I stick my hand out to Roisin to help her onto the dock, and she takes it.

That's a good sign.

I pay the captain using a phone transfer, then tug Roisin into town. "Stassi and Liam are fine."

She sags with relief. "How did you find out?"

"Elio. He sent one of his lieutenants over."

"That was fast."

The boat ride had been hours long. "I imagine they were nearby."

Roisin sighs. "Where are they?"

"Don't know," I grumble. "Don't care."

Roisin looks back at me with confusion.

I scan the surrounding town. It's bigger than the last one, but still tiny. "We need to go find somewhere to sleep, and something to eat. I need to pull out some cash, and then we need to get to Switzerland."

She blinks. "Switzerland?"

"Keep your voice down," I whisper. "Yes."

"Marco. How the hell is that going to help?"

"It will keep you safe," I growl. Why can't she fucking see that?

Roisin shakes her head. "I need to stay here, in Ireland. I can't be a fugitive. And I certainly can't look like I'm guilty enough to run to a country that doesn't always play nice with extradition."

Fucking hell. "Roisin. You will be going to Switzerland if it's the last thing we fucking do."

"No, I won't," she says.

With that, she strides away.

About to grind my molars into dust, I follow her.

Irritating woman.

Why can't she see that I'm just trying to keep her safe?

I catch up to Roisin, who is walking ahead of me quickly. "Roisin. Be reasonable. If we stay in Ireland, that's what they're hoping for. They're going to hunt you down until they find you, and then you won't have anywhere to go."

"We don't even know who they are!" she practically shouts.

Shit.

I grab her arm, ignoring her squeak of protest, and tug her into an alley.

Roisin starts to raise her voice, but I cover her mouth quickly. When she raises a hand to smack me, I shake my head. "Stop," I whisper, my voice a harsh scrape against the cold sea air. "Just stop. Just wait, Roisin."

She narrows her eyes. Her chest is heaving, and I do my best to keep our gazes locked, so I don't look down at her very tempting breasts.

Finally, she nods, and I lower my hand.

"Think about it. Seriously. If we're constantly running from them, whoever they are, then we're not going to be able to do anything to figure this out. Moretti isn't stupid. I'm sure he's already looking up the records of whoever left the dock, and he knows our destination. It's only a matter of time. We need to stay one step ahead of him, then when we're safe at the safehouse in Lugano, we can do some digging."

Roisin hisses, the sound a laugh that's desperate and claws at my chest. "A safe house? Really?"

"Really."

Roisin shakes her head. "Look, I appreciate the offer, Marco. But this isn't your fight. You made it crystal clear what we are to each other, and I'm not asking you to risk any more. If you want to leave, you can leave, but I'm staying."

"Roisin..."

Footsteps, echoing through the alley, spur me to action.

I tuck Roisin into an alcove. It smells foul back here, but the smell of trash might keep whoever is in the alley away. When they keep coming, I do something else instead.

I duck my head down, tugging the fishy blanket that Roisin is covered in up around her ears, and I kiss her.

Somehow, some fucking how, I can't keep my lips off of her. It doesn't matter if we're in mortal danger or if we smell like fish, the only thing that I can do when it comes to her is keep her safe.

With a kiss.

At first, it's just a kiss. She's mad at me, so her lips are tight under mine. Gently, I bring the sides of my hands up to cup her face.

I want Roisin back.

I want the woman who I kissed in the shower. I want the woman who I kissed, who tasted like the ocean and the sun. I want the woman that I spent my days and nights with in a tiny cabin on the Irish coast.

I want the only thing I've ever wanted for myself.

The one thing that hasn't belonged to my family, the one obligation I've never felt like I had to fill. I wanted Roisin before I knew who she was.

And damn it.

I'm going to have her.

I tug her hair, noting how the tangles make it easy for me to burrow my fingers against her scalp. She softens under my hands, her lips opening with a breathy moan that I capture as I lap at the sound of her sigh.

I know the moment she loses control too.

The blanket drops, forgotten as she and I kiss. Her legs wobble, and I put my knee in between them. The position means that she's kind of half-standing against my leg, her back to the wall, my thigh between hers.

And when she starts to rub herself, slightly, on the hard length of my thigh, I practically purr with joy.

The kiss deepens. It becomes something different entirely. It's the kiss that we shared all those nights ago, the one that was interrupted. It's the one in the shower that I hated myself for.

It's every kiss I wish I'd given her, over and over again.

Roisin gasps, and I growl. I want her like this. Needy. Open. Wanting me. She scrapes her nails along my scalp, and I want to growl like a fucking tiger at the sensation.

She's perfect.

She's mine.

I have to keep her safe.

Roisin's fully rubbing her hot center on my thigh now, and I'm as hard as a fucking rock inside my thick denim jeans.

I want her.

I want her more than I've ever wanted anything in my fucking life...

"Well. This is not exactly how I was expecting this would go."

A woman's voice, with a lilting Irish accent, breaks through the fog of my lust.

Roisin shoves me away, peering from around me at the person in the alley. I turn.

There's a woman there. She's about Roisin's height. Come to think of it, she has Roisin's tangle of hair as well.

My world shatters when Roisin says one word.

"Mum?"

14

ROISIN

My mother is standing in the alley.

There's absolutely no doubt in my mind. It's the mother I remember, but a decade and a half older. Her hair is the same, the brown of her eyes the same. Her skin looks older; there are marks there that have never been there before.

Wrinkles. Lines. Spots. Things I don't remember.

But no scars.

That I can see.

She's got her arms folded across her chest, and her head tilted. I step away from Marco, who keeps trying to stand in front of me.

The expression on her face isn't anger, or loss, or surprise, even.

It's a kind of mild amusement that reminds me of the time I'd covered a hallway in a crayon mural when I was four.

Having one's mum catch them making out is never good.

But finding her like this, while I'm wrapped up in Marco's arms?

I feel so shocked, I'm numb.

"Well, my little Rosie. I'm glad you're okay."

My jaw is on the floor. "Mum. Is… are you…"

A smile breaks across her face then.

"Aye, darling. 'Tis me."

I stumble forward and fall into her arms.

When I smell her familiar perfume, violets and vanilla, I start to cry.

I don't know how long I spend blubbering in that foul alley, wrapped up in my mother's arms. But by the time I've cried everything I have, her hands gently stroking my hair, I feel a thousand years older.

I feel empty.

But mostly I feel…

Confused.

I pull back. "How are you alive?" I whisper.

Sadness tugs at my mum's face, pulling the corners of her eyes down. Instinctively, I want to tell her that it's going to be okay. That I can take care of whatever is bothering her.

But, I can't. I don't know what's making her sad. And now that all my tears have left my body, I sense something else, simmering deep underneath all the sorrow and worry I've carried for years.

Anger.

"This isn't a conversation for a place like this," she murmurs, her eyes darting around the alley. "Come. Bring your young man, and let's go back to my place."

I resist the urge to tell her that he's not mine. Marco and I aren't beholden to each other, in any way.

Except, apparently, for the fact that we can't stop kissing each other.

I can't think about that right now.

If I think about kissing Marco again, I'm going to melt into a puddle of emotions and I don't think I'm ever going to be able to put myself back together.

You need to stop kissing him.

I'll figure that out later.

My mum turns, and I look at Marco. His face is tight, a silent question etched into his brown eyes.

Do you trust her?

"I think I do," I whisper.

His nostrils flare. I can tell he's about to protest.

I shake my head. "She's my mum, Marco."

"I don't understand."

Mum stands at the edge of the alley, waiting. I look at Marco. "Kieran... my dad... they did something to her. Or that's what I thought. It's why I lived with them. My dad found me, and my mom had to give me to him."

Marco's lips thin. "I don't know."

"She's my mum, Marco," I plead.

I hate the desperation in my voice.

He looks at her, then gives a sharp snort.

"Will you go to Switzerland after this?"

I don't have any intention of leaving Ireland. However, I need to go with her. I need answers.

So I look at Marco, and I lie straight to his face.

"Yes."

Mum leads us to a townhouse, one of the little sea-facing ones that are stacked like rainbow-colored blocks vertically along the Irish shore. It's quaint; the town is small, and the townhouse is tiny. Marco has to duck to get through the door, and I can tell instantly that he doesn't like the inside.

Too fucking bad.

I also know what his protests will be. It's not easy to defend. You can set the entire row of houses on fire to get to this one. There's only one way in and out. I know them, because I have them too.

This is screaming—according to all my instincts—*dangerous*, but I can't stop.

She's my *mum*.

And I haven't seen her since I was ten years old.

Inside, Marco is loath to separate from me. Mum seats me on a worn couch, looking at Marco, who is looming like an overgrown crow.

"I'll make us some tea," she finally says.

It feels so normal. Like something a mother would do, if they were meeting their daughter's partner for the first time.

She disappears, and Marco gives me a sharp nod.

"I'm going to check out the house. If anything happens, scream," he whispers.

I roll my eyes. "I don't need to do that."

He gives me a meaningful look. But I like that he thinks I can take care of myself.

I think.

My feelings about Marco are in turmoil. I'm relieved that he found out what happened to my brother and Stassi. I'm annoyed that he keeps trying to push me to go to Switzerland. I'm relieved that he thinks I can be alone in a dangerous environment, even if it is with my mother.

I'm annoyed that he thinks I need to scream for help.

It's a rollercoaster. One that isn't helped by the fact that every time he kisses me, my brain becomes completely scrambled and I can't remember who I am.

Or what I'm doing.

My mum comes back, a classic tea service, chipped cups and all, on a tray. Her hands shake, slightly, as she sets it down.

Marco drifts back in, ready to hover behind my shoulder, a threatening shadow.

She gives him a look. "Tea?"

"No," he rumbles.

Her lips tilt up in a smile. "Ah. American."

"I hate tea. And coffee," he grumbles.

Well. That's not true. He drank plenty of tea when I made it for him at the cottage…

"I was wondering, um…" my mom gives Marco a meaningful look, waiting for him to supply his name.

"Marco," he grunts.

"Marco. If I might have a moment alone with my daughter?"

"Whatever you say to Roisin, you can say in front of me," he rasps.

Her eyebrows raise. "I think she's the one who is supposed to tell me that."

There's steel under her voice.

Marco's jaw clenches, but I wave him off. "It's fine, Mum. Whatever you want to say, Marco can hear."

Her eyes flash to him. "What's his last name, love?"

I'm not about to give away that Marco is a DeLuca. For some reason, part of me wants to hold that back. The part of my brain that's been conditioned for years by Interpol kicks in.

She might not tell me everything if she knows Marco is mafia too.

"Smith," he supplies.

I don't react.

Her eyes narrow. "Marco Smith? You're expecting me to believe a man who is clearly more bloody Italian than a box of pasta at Tesco is named Marco Smith?"

"Family name. Dad's English," he says with a hint of a sneer.

"Lord have mercy. He even talks like one of them," she sighs.

"Talks like who, Mum?" I ask.

My mother looks at me. She hands me a cup of tea, and I sip.

"He talks like your father."

The tea freezes in my hand.

Mum sighs. "Well, I can't say I didn't fall for it too. I don't know who your family is, boy," she gives him a look that's pure venom. "But I assure you, if you hurt my daughter, then there will be hell to pay."

"Mum. From who?" I whisper.

She shuts her eyes.

"Well, I suppose you'll want some answers then."

The teacup rattles slightly against the saucer as I set it down.

My mom nods. "I made a bargain with your father, the night… before you were born. If I bore him a child, I could choose which portion of their life I wanted. A ten-year span. I chose the first ten, because I had met men like him before. I was in university at the time, and I studied child development. The first ten years of a child's life are the most important, you know," she says, her voice taking on a flat tone. "It's when you learn the skills that make you into the person you are."

I breathe. "Why the hell did my father do this to all his children?"

She shrugs. "He was an evil man, love. Evil men love to destroy things."

The fact that he couldn't just raise a child, all on his own, isn't shocking to me. William MacAntyre was a horrific man.

Well. I suppose he did raise Kieran.

Marco, behind me, grunts. "What do you mean, made a bargain."

My mom looks down, her fingers twisting the scrap of fabric that she'd been using as a napkin.

Her silence makes the hair on the back of my neck stand up. "Mum..."

"The bargain was... God. Just know that I love you, Roisin. My Rosie. I've always loved you. Every second of it. And when I walked away, it killed me," she says.

There are tears in her eyes.

"What do you mean, walked away?" I whisper.

My mum looks down at the tea service. "The bargain was... he paid me to have you. To have a child. I got to pick which of the child's life I wanted for ten years. I got to decide, and I decided the first ten, and then after that..." she stops, her throat thick with tears.

"After that, the terms of the contract were fulfilled," Marco growls from behind me.

The realization of what's being said sinks into me.

"You... sold me?"

My mum's crying now, tears falling down her face. "It wasn't... I didn't... it was already done..."

"But you left me with him," I say.

My voice sounds small. So, so incredibly small.

"I... it was the contract," she whispers.

"You could have fought him. We could have left."

They're not suggestions. They're accusations. I know what I would have done in her position. She was fully aware of who my father was. Of what she was doing.

She made a deal with my father to bear him a child. An heir, of some kind. Someone for him to destroy, just like he'd destroyed Liam and Killian.

She made me because he paid her to.

Then she sold me, when the time came.

My heart, which broke the night she brought me to him, feels like it's shattering all over again.

My mom looks up, her fingers stilling. "He was *William MacAntyre*, love. He was the bogeyman, the monster that everyone around here has always been afraid of. I knew, without a shadow of a doubt, that he or one of his evil sons would kill me."

I can't believe what I'm hearing. I sit back, the tea nearly forgotten. "You knew about Kieran?"

She snorts. "Everyone knew about Kieran. He was only a teenager, but he was vile," she whispers.

"And you left me with him anyway?"

Her eyes get round. "Roisin..."

I stand, looking at Marco. "I think I'd like to go now."

My mother starts to protest. "No, love, I'm so sorry. I just... when I saw your face on the news, I decided to start heading back toward the manor, just to see if you were there..."

"We're a several hour's boat ride from that place," I say dully. "Were you planning on staying here forever?"

She shakes her head. "No, it's not like that, darling, please, you have to believe me…"

"I don't," I say sharply.

She inhales.

"I want to go. Please don't follow me. Don't contact me. And don't ever try to find me again."

I let Marco hold the door for me. I step outside, into what's become a freezing coastal storm. I look back at Marco.

"Take me to fucking Switzerland."

15

MARCO

Elio's safe house in Lugano is the type of place that doesn't feel real. Positioned as it is in the mountains, overlooking a stunning lake, every building looks like something out of a damn postcard.

I can't help the fact that my eyes get pretty damn big every time we go around a curve in the winding road to get up to it.

For two people with no passports and no money, it was shockingly easy to get here.

It helps that I've spent the past decade and a half developing a network of favors that, at this point, I'm cashing in at a rapid pace.

From Ireland, we hopped a boat with a French gang out of Marseille. Jean-Luc is one shifty fucker, but he knows how to dodge customs like it's no one's business. His boss, an even more dirty and sketchy Frenchman, practically built the smuggling routes between Marseille and Africa. If there's someone who can get you anywhere, it's them, and when I threatened to unearth the information I had on Jean-Luc's favorite aunt's lavender farm in Provence, including how many pesticides go into the supposedly pesticide-free flowers, they begrudgingly offered us passage.

From there, the car was an easy solution. I pay a group of Algerian teenagers a living wage, which they mostly take to their families, to bring back information on the comings and goings of Marseille. They located a car that Jean-Luc had recently lifted, and we did the original owners the favor of stealing it right back. When we abandoned it in Annemasse, I made sure to call the Interpol tip line, so that whoever the owner of a beautiful black Ferrari is, they can have it back now.

It does me no favors with the French, but they rely on Elio and the Rossi's to bring them luxury goods to smuggle, so they'll get over it. I made a note to tell Elio to raise their bonus, just slightly, and when he asked why, I told him about the Ferrari.

He had been pissed, of course, but Elio is very rarely happy.

From Annemasse, it was easy to get the train to Geneva. Then to Bern. Then to Lugano.

And now, we're in a car that I rented, with passports Elio had sent to a locker in the train station. The money was here already, hidden in a bank account that I inherited when my father died, and while I'm sure Elio's curious about the cash I'm using, this particular account wasn't part of our merge.

I'm also sure he's asking my siblings what the hell is going on.

But, they don't know either.

After my parents' death, finding my mother's journals had been debilitating. I know my mom, and my dad, in a way that none of my siblings do.

In a way that no child should probably understand about their parents, to be honest.

My parents loved each other, but it was recent. Their relationship began as a business arrangement; it was broken up by the time my mother left, and was more or less involuntarily held at the family home of Iannis Drakos.

It was voluntary, I think, until Iannis turned out to be a dick.

Either way, she escaped and came back pregnant with my half-brother Dino.

But my father was not an easy man to get along with.

To some extent, I understand that this is because he was a product of his times. Living as they did, scraping a living after the legacy of leaving Italy, the experience of coming to America in the early 1900s… all of that gets written not just into a person, but into a family. A bloodline.

And pain that has a way of echoing through generations.

My father's way of running the De Luca family was exactly what he had always known. Hard. Lots of people were shot if they didn't do things my dad's way. My grandfather and uncle were probably better suited to run the organization than he was. Until stupid Jacob Capano lost the case that indicted both of them, and the RICOH charges finally stuck.

It wasn't his fault. Capano is a good lawyer. He never really recovered from that case, but it would have been nearly impossible to beat.

When my uncle and grandfather went to jail, my dad wasn't ready to run the De Lucas.

Which meant that between him and my mom, things were rough.

And I know that.

But I don't need my siblings to.

They can keep the vision of my parents as in love with each other. Dancing at Elio and Caterina's first engagement party. The gentle kiss my dad had placed on my mom's head, the way they'd held each other.

The perfection of the night that they'd died.

I'll hold their darkness. I'll keep their secrets.

But holding it, I think, might be slowly killing me.

When we round the final bend to the safe house, I hear Roisin suck in a breath. "Wow," she murmurs.

I nod. "I know."

Elio's family doesn't skimp when it comes to vacation homes.

We park the car inside the subterranean garage, and I check to make sure there's no one on the street before I unlock the door. Inside, the house is stunning. It overlooks the lake, and it's set back from the main town slightly. Highly defensible, and I boot up all the security systems as Roisin peers out the living room window.

I stand next to her. "I'll have some food sent here in a few hours. Do you need—"

"No," she snaps.

I watch as Roisin walks away, her shoes snapping on the floor.

What the hell have I done now?

16

ROISIN

It's all too much.

The house. The drive. The way that Marco just... took care of everything.

I thought I knew him. I really thought that I at least had an idea of who Marco De Luca was. After all, I spent the better half of a year living with him. I thought I knew details about him, like what made him smile or how competent he was at fixing things like a silly garden gate.

It turns out, I don't know Marco De Luca at all.

He's smooth.

Watching him bully a notorious French gangster. Watching him steal a fucking Ferrari. Watching his hands on the steering wheel as he drove it up twisting roads in the Alps, the mountains on either side of us dropping away into the valley floor below, while he didn't so much as break a sweat...

If I had tried to apprehend Marco De Luca, just on the street, as a regular criminal, I wouldn't have stood a chance.

The fact that he was in my custody for so long, while also being *this* type of a person, tells me one thing.

Marco allowed himself to remain in my little cottage. He chose to be there.

Because the man who smoothly produced two perfect fake passports and a boatload of cash, the man who's been sitting and monitoring a security system for the past two days, who has cooked me dinners worthy of a Michelin star, quietly leaving the plate outside of the room that I've decided is mine, isn't a man who can be contained.

I was right, all those times when I was overwhelmed by him.

Marco De Luca is a force of nature.

And I never stood a chance at containing him.

I know that I should take the time to dig into who is trying to frame me. It's been three days since we arrived in Lugano, and basically all I've done is eat, and sleep, and mope.

I feel like a bloody worm.

But, I'm also… hurting.

I don't know if it's the fact that I've just left everything for so long, or if learning about my mother broke me. But I feel, literally, broken. Every time I move, something inside my chest seems to tweak. Every time I take a breath, it hurts.

I literally think that I've been broken by this.

My mother *sold me*.

The whole reason that I exist, on this planet, is that she made a deal with a literal devil. William MacAntyre, as she said, was an evil man.

And she not only made a deal with him, but when it was time to pay up, she did.

I wasn't born out of love, or even some kind of mistake. I was very much planned.

The plan, however, was to create me so that I could be some kind of asset of my father's. Like my brothers.

God almighty, are there other children out there like me? Creations that my father paid for, but he never came to collect?

I could ask my mother but...

I won't.

I don't know if I'll ever talk to her again. I don't know if I will want to. Knowing that she willingly followed everything my father did, that she not only played right into his hands, but developed plans with him?

It's more than I can bear.

I am not a mistake. I'm not even a love-child, or something stupid like that. I'm no happy accident, and my mother wasn't taken from me.

I was a cultivated plant.

And she sold me willingly.

The thoughts make the spot in my chest ache again. I'm past crying, it would seem, because while I feel the urge to, there are no tears that come out of my eyes.

Just emptiness.

Sorrow.

That's what this feels like.

Sorrow, and loss, and a complete and total change in the world as I knew it.

The sound of footsteps in the hall draws my attention. I don't listen to them, not really. It's just very quiet in here. I can hear Marco shuffling around the house, so I know when he's working in the computer room or when he's making food.

I just don't care anymore.

Marco knocks, as always, to open the door.

As always, I do nothing.

I wait for him to put the plate on the dresser, the soft clink of the porcelain on wood my sign to wait until the door snicks shut before I get up to try whatever pasta dish he's decided to craft today.

But there isn't one.

I turn over, blinking at the bright light of the door. "Marco?" I ask, my voice hoarse.

"Good morning."

He's holding something in his hand, and I can see a croissant placed on the dresser in the usual spot. I sit up slightly.

"What's that?"

He tosses it at me.

It's a swimsuit. A bikini, actually, and the thought of wearing it out on the lake while it's this cold makes me wince.

"What's this for?"

"Put it on."

"Marco..."

"Put it on, or I will put it on for you," he rumbles.

The door shuts.

I stare at the bikini. It's my size, which is unsurprising, and it's black. Also unsurprising. Marco isn't exactly a colorful guy, so it stands to reason that his taste is similarly morose.

I don't want to do whatever this is. I don't...

"Put it on or I'll put it on for you," he growls through the door.

"It's freezing out there," I snap back.

"We're not going to the lake in the winter."

"Where are we going?"

"Put it on, and you'll see," he snarls.

Ugh.

My hands move, almost of their own accord, out to the bikini. Marco's supplied me with an entire wardrobe since I got here. I have a shirt that I could cover this up with, so I don't just prance around in a bikini wherever we're going.

"In ten seconds, Roisin, if you don't have it on..."

Insufferable man. "Fine. I'm going," I yell.

I'm so annoyed with him, I am going to wear the biggest, baggiest set of clothes over this that I can find.

Ten seconds later, I whip open the door, covered in a giant sweatsuit and wearing the damn bikini. My hair is tugged into a messy bun, and I haven't brushed my teeth.

It's a clear symbol for *wherever we're going, I'm going to go but I protest.*

Marco doesn't even bat an eye. He grabs my hand, and tugs me toward the garage. When I ask where we're going, he turns and winks.

Winks.

"You'll see. Do you trust me?"

Bloody hell.

The answer is still fucking yes.

The car ride is several hours. We weave deep into the mountains. Marco chose a different vehicle this time, a rugged Range Rover that looks like it can conquer entire nations on its own. Eventually, he takes a turn up a tiny path that looks more goat path than road, cranking on the vehicle's four-wheel drive system. The Range Rover snarls, leaping up the tiny road, and eventually I see a sign.

Bagni di Craveggia.

Accompanied by a little icon that has a circle, indicating water, and three wavy lines above it.

I frown. "What's that?"

"You'll see."

I'm still angry at Marco, and I don't want to ask him any follow up questions. So instead, I stare out the window and try to see if I can figure it out myself.

When we finally pull up to a mostly empty parking lot and a rocky lake, I finally give up. "What the hell, Marco," I snap. "Where the hell are we?"

"I told you it was a surprise."

He starts to unload the car, and I hop down. My feet are in boots, which I am glad I chose, because the cold seeps in through them. I look down at the lake, noting the ripples in the water...

Wait.

This high up, at this time of year, this lake should be solid ice. Completely frozen.

But it's not frozen.

On top of that, it's steaming...

"A hot spring?"

Marco's smile makes something in my chest loosen. "I knew my smart girl was in there somewhere."

My girl?

The comment leaves me momentarily stunned, and I watch Marco grab a bag of towels, with a wrapped package that looks suspiciously like a wine bottle, and head toward the spring.

Dumbfounded, I follow.

The spring is stunning. The mountains around us are hush, quiet with a blanket of snow. There's no one else here, and I have no doubt there won't be. To access this road, we practically had to use a car that can go over nearly any terrain. Not a lot of people will be able to follow us, not in the winter.

Plus, it's starting to snow.

A couple of flakes drift down, evaporating once they hit the heat of the water. Marco uses a rock to set up a little tent, covering a space so the snow doesn't fall on it. He places our bag there, keeping it dry and free from snow, then starts to pull off his shirt.

I stare.

Marco De Luca is a beautiful man. I've always known that. But the number of times that I've seen him without a shirt are few.

And now, I can see a lot.

Dense muscle rolls over his broad frame. Marco is shorter than his brothers, but definitely packed with the type of muscle that looks like it's from another time entirely. He looks like he should be lifting a broadsword or straddling a destrier.

Not flexing those biceps, casually, to pop the top of a champagne bottle.

His skin is a very deep olive color. In the summer, I know that it bronzes, absorbing the sun like a sponge. His tattoos aren't prolific like some men I've seen, but he has enough to make me want to touch them. The span of his broad pecs is covered in hair, but he's somehow tamed it so that it looks… groomed.

Sexy.

Like I want to scrape my nails along it.

Marco takes his pants off next, and I instinctively turn. He laughs.

"I'm going in. There's champagne for you here on the ledge," he murmurs.

I peek, I will admit, as he moves toward the spring.

Damn.

With an ass like that, it's a wonder he can put on pants at all.

Cautiously, I strip as well, then take the glass. The snow on the path feels like it's burning, it's so cold, and I scoot quickly to the spring.

Without looking to see if Marco is watching, I step down into the rocky spring.

The water is hot. It feels lovely, especially with the snow drifting down and the cold on my shoulders. I drink the champagne, and I feel the knot in my chest loosen slightly.

I can feel Marco watching me from across the spring, but I can't look at him.

Not yet.

I sigh.

"So. This is your plan to... what? Get me naked and wet?"

"No," he rumbles. "I just wanted to see you live again."

That opens my eyes.

Marco stares at me, all intensity across the steam of the spring. He nods. "Finding out all that about your parents is terrible."

I look down.

"When my parents died, I found my mom's journal. She wrote in it about how she didn't love my dad. The ways that he was cruel to her."

I look at Marco.

He's staring at me. "Eventually, they loved each other. But not at first. And not after she had a son by another man."

"Dino," I confirm.

He nods.

"Why are you telling me this?"

He shrugs. "Just thought you'd want to know you aren't alone."

It makes me feel...

The knot in my chest loosens further.

"You know, the whole reason I joined Interpol was to find my mum," I whisper.

Marco's gaze snaps to me, laser-like.

"I thought that she was in witness protection, or something. That if I was just in Interpol, and I worked in a similar agency, she'd come up. Eventually."

He doesn't say anything.

"My whole life. Literally all of it. Was a lie," I whisper.

"No."

I glance at Marco.

"It wasn't a lie. You are who you are because of their choices. But you built yourself around the framework they gave. You are still yourself, Roisin. Even if the adults in your world lied to you."

I hadn't thought of it that way.

The thought turns over in my mind. Everything feels like it's in turmoil.

And the handsome man in the hot spring is part of it.

I look at him. "Why are you doing this?" I ask again.

Marco narrows his eyes. "What do you mean?"

"You hate me. I betrayed you, remember? I lied to you," I say. The words taste bitter on my tongue, and I sip champagne to get rid of them.

Marco's eyes could cut through stone. "You did betray me. And I do hate that."

"So why are you doing all this?" I gesture to the hot spring.

He hesitates. I can see the wheels of his mind turning. Finally, he gives me a sharp nod.

"Because I need you to be happy more than I hate that you lied to me."

CHAPTER 17: MARCO

I'm not sure why I'm being honest with Roisin.

Well, actually, I do know why. I'm generally honest. I don't tell lies to people.

But sometimes, I hold the truth very close to my chest.

The fact that I'm not doing that now, that I'm being open with her about why I'm being so damn nice to her, is unusual.

But it feels right.

Maybe it's the fact that drinking champagne at high altitude hits me a little faster than it should. Maybe it's the heat of the spring, or the way Roisin's body looks, slick and glistening, in the water.

Maybe it's the fact that I think I might be losing a grasp on everything that I thought was important to me.

But I literally drove hours to this spring, just to make Roisin smile. I'll be damned if I don't accomplish that.

She studies me, her green eyes darker, reflecting the gathering dusk and the heaviness of the clouds overhead.

God damn it. All I want is to kiss her.

Somehow, I can't stay away from this woman. I want to touch her constantly. I want to make her smile. The little wrinkle between her eyebrows when she's sad makes me feel like I want to fight someone. She's been lying in her room, alone, for days.

If I thought it would help, I'd kill her father all over again.

I toyed with the thought of kidnapping her mother and bringing her, just to tell her to fix it, to fix my Roisin, but ultimately I'm not sure that it would be effective. Roisin doesn't seem to want to talk to her mother, not after all the information she dropped, anyway.

So instead, I looked up a hot spring. And I planned a fucking picnic. And we're staying at a little cabin tonight that's nearby, and I packed her a goddamn bag full of clothes that aren't even remotely sexy, but they're comfortable and soft.

And every second of that process, I couldn't fucking believe myself.

Because every time I did something to take care of Roisin, the chaos inside me settled slightly.

Watching her in her room, I felt completely powerless. Feeling powerless makes me...

It makes me feel like I have some kind of buzzing under my skin. Like I can't settle down until I figure out whatever's bothering her.

I don't like to feel powerless.

After Dino was born, my mother didn't leave her room for almost half a year. I was the one who stepped in to hold my crying brother. Who tried to get my mom to pay attention to us.

I was four.

Four, holding my infant brother, who screamed like a motherfucker.

So seeing Roisin, day after day, refuse to get up, it fucking hurt.

That's why. The childhood trauma. No other reason.

The water in the spring sloshes slightly, bringing me back to reality. Roisin nods. "Well, I guess I can accept that."

"You don't have an option," I growl. "I wanted you to feel better. So feel better."

"You do know that you don't have the ability to control my feelings, right?"

I snort. "I can't control them, but I can be the reason they change."

"That sounds manipulative, Marco."

I pause. "What?"

Roisin sighs. She sips the champagne. "Do you want my feelings to change because you're worried about me, or because me having feelings makes you feel uncomfortable?"

I genuinely do not know how to answer that question.

Roisin nods. "That's what I thought. Because if you care about me, and you are trying to cheer me up because you do, it's sweet. But if you're trying to make me feel better because you can't handle someone else's feelings, and it makes you feel out of control, that's enmeshment and you should probably see someone for it."

"Enmeshment?"

She nods. "Poor emotional boundaries. Someone who was brought up to take care of theirs, their parents, might be enmeshed. Families that lacked distinctions between parents and children. That kind of thing."

"How do you know this, Dr. Phil?"

She laughs. "I went to therapy, dummy. For years. Because I lived with Kieran MacAntyre, and I fucking needed therapy to get past that."

I don't have a response to that.

She sighs. "You know, Kieran told me that he knew where my mom was. And that he'd kill her if I tried to leave to find her."

The water makes a slight noise as I shuffle around. "What?"

"My dad didn't know where my mom was. Probably because he didn't think that far in the future. I think it bothered him. He'd made this bargain with her, she dropped me off with him, collected her payday, and was gone. Kieran told me that if I left to try and find her, he'd kill her."

"Do you think he knew?"

She barks out a laugh. "No. I think Kieran was just cruel. I think he liked holding his new little sister in some kind of hold. I think he wanted to torture me."

I growl, thinking of how terrible Kieran was to her. I'd kill that fucker again, if I could.

Then, I tilt my head and study her. "How did you come to live with your father and Kieran?"

She sighs. "When I was about ten, my mum told me it was time to finally meet my dad. I was thrilled. We lived in Dublin, so heading out to the manor house was basically the longest trip I'd ever taken. When we got there, my dad just... nodded. Like I was acceptable. He and my mum went to talk, and Kieran appeared. He was nice, I guess, at first. He's so much older than me, he seemed like a god. He gave me candy and kept me in the kitchen. My mum and I slept in what would become my room. When I woke up, she was gone. And I stayed there."

Jesus. "That's awful, Roisin."

She shakes her head. Little drops of water cascade out from her hair, and I watch them splatter into the water around us. "I mean it makes a whole lot of sense now. I really thought that when my mum left, she'd run away. That somehow she'd escaped, or she was just going to come back for me later. When I got older, I wondered if Kieran or my dad had killed her that night. But this was the whole reason I became an Interpol officer. I thought that maybe she'd made it to safety. That she was trying to find me too, and she was just in hiding somewhere. Biding her time until it was time for her to find me. So I thought I'd make it easier, and join the police, so that I could find her first," Roisin murmurs.

"No wonder you're so fucked up over this."

She nods. "This isn't just some news, Marco. It's not something that's like... disappointing, but not a big deal, to learn. I built my entire life around the assumption that my mum was out there, in hiding. That my father, or Kieran, had done something awful to her to separate us. I became a police officer, I sold information to Liam, all so that I could find her," she says.

Her voice is desperate. It cracks, like something inside of her is fracturing.

I didn't, however, miss that she said *I sold information to Liam.*

"She wasn't forced away from me. She wasn't hurt, or captured, or anything like that. She chose to walk away. Because she sold me. I wasn't some kind of... product of love or anything like that. My mother made a deal with my father, and she sold me as part of it," she spits out bitterly.

I shake my head. "It's all fucked up."

"That's it?"

Looking at Roisin, I shrug. 'What else do you want?"

Her mouth opens, then closes. "I don't know. Maybe for you to be mad? Or just... I don't know," she admits.

"There are times when things happen to us and we can't do anything about them. You were a kid. You had absolutely no influence in your mother's decision. You didn't choose to be conceived under a contract, you didn't choose to be brought up the way you were. There's nothing you can do about that. There never was," I rumble.

Roisin rolls her eyes. "Look who's doing therapy now."

"All I'm saying is that life is fucking short and you only have so much time and energy. Don't spend it looking at everything that could have happened. Don't waste it on people who did what they did, if you don't want to. You're a grown-ass adult. If you want to keep talking to your mother, and feel that same shame or anger or whatever it is you're feeling, do it. If you want to cut her out, do it. Either way, you get to choose."

"Is that what you'd do?" she retorts. Her cheeks are flushed, and I can see her lips pressed together in anger.

Roisin narrows her eyes at me. "You'd just cut someone out?"

"Yes," I nod.

She rolls her eyes. "Whatever. I've seen the lengths you'll go to for your family."

"As would you," I snap.

Roisin freezes, the cup halfway to her lips. "What?"

"You, apparently, would do things for family too. You just said that you sold information to Liam. What information, Roisin?" I rasp.

My own anger is building. If she sold me out, if that was the reason for that day in the cottage...

"Oh shut the fuck up," she barks at me. "I was feeding Liam information from my job so that he would help me keep looking for my mum. God damn it Marco, not everything is about you!" she shouts.

She punctuates her shout with a champagne glass, tossed directly at my head. I duck, and it descends into the spring. Roisin makes an angry little noise, then turns on her heel, stomping up and out of the stone steps, toward the Range Rover.

I watch her go, noting how the water slides down off of her perfect ass.

Fuck, she didn't even stop to get a towel or the sandals I'd brought to cover her feet. With the near inch of snow on the ground, she's going to freeze.

Goddamn it.

"Don't run away from me like that, Roisin!" I bellow. I slosh up and out of the spring, grabbing the bag of towels as I go. "You don't get to run away from me!"

"I do whatever I want!" she tosses over her shoulder. "You're not my keeper, Marco DeLuca!"

"Like hell I'm not!" I growl.

Roisin might be athletic, but she's short. Without breaking into a somewhat undignified run, she'll never escape my longer legs.

I use that to my full advantage. I grab one of the towels out of the bag, then get it in both of my hands. I come up behind her and bundle her in the towel, wrapping it around her arms and torso.

She kicks and hisses like an angry cat, but I just wrap the towel tighter. I scoop Roisin up, tossing her over my shoulder while I stalk up to the Range Rover.

Unlocking the door, I gently set her on the seat. Her limbs are still covered by the towel, and she looks at me like she'd bite me, if she could.

I blink at her. "You were going to sit on the seat dripping wet. It ruins the leather."

"I fucking hope so!" she shrieks at me.

I shut the door, then go to retrieve our bag.

A smile tugs at the edges of my mouth.

Roisin is pissed. Genuinely raging angry.

And it's so much better than her being locked away behind bars of sadness and fear.

By the time I pick everything up and we're on the way again, Roisin has calmed somewhat. She refuses to speak to me, which I find I'm also annoyed by. It makes me want to reach out and hold her. Ask if she's okay.

Do anything except sit and be surrounded by her stony silence.

She does notice, however, when we don't continue on the road back to the lake house.

"If you're taking me somewhere to kill me, De Luca, you should know I won't go down easy."

I can't help it. I laugh. "If I wanted to kill you, I could have done it in a million different ways by now, Rosin."

She snorts. "You'd wait until it was perfectly to your advantage."

My heart twists a little, but not because she's wrong.

"I'm not used to being so predictable," I murmur.

"Well. I guess not everyone would notice," Roisin responds.

But she does notice.

The mountain road gets steeper, and I'm grateful for the SUV's off-road capabilities. At this point, we're practically plowing through snow, and when we finally roll up to the little cabin I found, the snow is coming down thick and heavy.

Roisin peers around, her face pinched in worry. "Okay seriously, Marco. I will haunt you forever if you kill me."

"It's a long way back to the lake house," I explain. "I didn't want to drive in the weather, and I wasn't sure how long we'd be at the spring, so I rented this."

Her eyebrow rises, and before she can say it, I cut her off.

"I used one of my aliases, and it's rented in cash. Honestly, Roisin. Do you think I'm an idiot?"

"Not the word I'd use, but the sentiment is true," she mutters.

I chuckle, then step out of the Range Rover. "Stay here until I come get you," I say to Roisin.

"I'm perfectly capable—"

"The snow is almost a foot deep. I'll carry you in, unless you want your feet to freeze?" I eye her naked toes meaningfully.

She wrinkles her nose. "Fine."

"Fine."

Shutting the door to the Rover, I trudge through the shin-high snow and punch in the key to the little rental. The cabin opens, and I quickly set the heat on. It's not a huge space. The main room flows into a kitchen, and just beyond I can see the door that leads to the bedroom and bathroom. The furniture is well-worn, but clean; a leather couch, thick rugs marking the space. It looks like the kitchen has been stocked too, which was one of the conditions of the rental.

Good.

There's a wood fireplace as well, but I'll have to mess with that later. I want Roisin in here and out of the cold before it gets too bad.

I retrieve her from the car, tucking her into my arms. She shivers, and I pull her closer. When we get into the cabin, I set her gently on the leather couch and wrap one of the blankets around her.

"I hope there's a shower. I smell like hot spring," Roisin murmurs.

"There's a shower, but I can't guarantee the water is hot."

She shrugs. "I'll see about that."

Roisin stands, and I wince as her perfect feet touch the cold wood floor. I want to sweep her up in my arms again so she doesn't have to walk across the cabin, but she's gone before I get the chance. I hear the shower start to run, and I return to the Range Rover for the rest of our supplies.

By the time I'm done, Roisin steps out from the shower, a luxurious looking towel wrapped around her body. Whoever put this place together did it with a kind of quiet luxury in mind, and it makes me feel a little settled.

If it had been a dump, I would have taken Roisin back to the lake house, weather be damned.

"I'd like some clothes, De Luca," she says.

I don't miss the breathiness in her voice, however.

My eyes follow the path of a water drop as it rolls down her neck, stopping right at the space of the hollow of her throat. She's so fucking pretty. The water drop stops right next to the little freckle that I've licked before.

I want to lick it again.

The taste of her skin...

"Marco. Clothes," she holds out one of her hands.

Robotically, I grab her bag and put it into her hands.

Roisin spins on her heel, heading back into the bathroom.

Leaving me, staring.

Wondering what the hell is wrong with me.

Eventually, Roisin comes out, fully dressed in so much clothing that I'm surprised she's not roasting hot.

Well. She is hot.

But I don't think she's going to admit that, and I don't mean it in terms of her temperature.

"Your turn," she waves at the shower.

I don't need to be reminded. However, instead of lingering like Roisin, I quickly move through and wash up, then exit to find her in the kitchen.

Something smells good.

"I hope you know I can't cook for shit," she mutters.

I smile. "I remember that."

Her green eyes flick to mine, then she looks down. "It's nothing special. You're stocked with sausages and the stuff for colcannon, so that's what I'm making."

"The cabin came with food," I say.

She stops chopping, looking down at the food with suspicion. "Just randomly? So how do you know it's not poisoned—"

I lean in, quickly sampling each one of the ingredients. Raw potatoes taste like shit, and the sausage is mostly cooked, but hot.

Roisin's jaw drops. "Marco! What if that had been poisoned!"

"Then the right person ate it," I say.

I mean it, too. I would fucking throw myself in front of a bus to save Roisin.

And I hope she knows it.

Since when?

Emotions scrape at the inside of my chest, and I turn, leaving the kitchen to sit on one of the rustic looking chairs balanced at the edge of the counter.

Having her here, her hair still damp, her skin fresh from the shower, her eyes furrowed in concentration, is too much like our time in her little seaside cottage.

And if I remember that time, the only word I have to describe it is…

Happy.

That was the last time that I truly was *happy*.

Not with my family. Not living under the thumb of my parents legacy.

In a seaside cottage, practically a prisoner.

With her.

"I don't want you doing stupid shit like that, Marco," she chides. "I think we both need to be a little more careful—"

Fuck it.

It takes me two seconds to cross the kitchen.

One to put my hands on either side of her, trapping her against the counter.

A half second to meet her eyes, to hover over her lips, to make sure that she's not saying no.

When the plush pink of her lips parts, I take my chance.

I dive in, and I kiss Roisin with every fucking pent up emotion that is tearing my heart apart.

Happy.

I want to be happy. I want this, and I'm not fucking strong enough to fight it anymore.

Roisin makes me happy.

And fuck me.

I want to make her happy too.

17

ROISIN

Lord help me, I should fight this kiss.

But I don't want to.

Marco might not want anything to do with me, but he brought me to a damn tiny crevice in the mountains to cheer me up. He carried me across the snow so that I didn't have to touch it. He made sure that the food I'm eating isn't poisoned, for Christ's sakes.

Marco De Luca might not want me, but he also has shown me more kindness and love than I've felt in years.

And I'm just a girl. I can't be expected to hold out under these conditions. On top of all of that, Marco walked out of the shower without a shirt on, and the curve of his muscles made me practically salivate with want.

I'm not strong enough to resist him. Complicated, messy, as awful as this is.

I want him. Pure, simple, and clean.

So I cave.

When his hand curls behind my neck, tugging my lips up to his, I moan and lean into it. The feeling of him pinning me to the counter should scare me. It should scare me a lot.

Except with Marco, I never feel trapped.

And while I've been scared plenty, he doesn't scare me.

I'm so tired of fighting this. Marco is like a drug, I know I'm an addict, and right now, I'm not strong enough to say no.

I kiss him with everything I've got.

It's not just a kiss. It's consuming. Marco's body is everywhere. The kitchen is small, absolutely, but it gets smaller by the second as his lips skate over my neck.

He smells good. Comforting.

Sexy.

I gasp when his hands scoop underneath my legs and lift me up onto the counter. I'm wearing some soft lounge pants and a tank top with a sweater over it, all selected from the bag that he packed for me.

Leaning back on the countertop, I shiver as Marco's hand finds its way under my shirt, tracing up the line of my stomach toward my breasts.

He moans when he finds out my choice (or lack thereof) in underwear.

"Jesus, Roisin. If I'd known..."

"You knew," I murmur. "You didn't pack me a comfy bra, so I had to make do."

Marco's eyes shoot up to mine, and I can tell that he's genuinely worried for a second. I lean forward and press a kiss between his eyebrows.

"I'm teasing you,' I whisper.

The brown of his eyes flashes. "If that's the decision you made, I'm throwing out every fucking bra I can find," he growls.

I laugh, but before I'm even really aware of it he has my shirt tugged up and over my head.

I shiver, but not because the air in the cabin is cold.

Marco's looking at me like he wants to devour me. Like I'm some kind of feast, spread out for him.

I tilt back, leaning on my elbows on the countertop.

"You," Marco growls, the sound of his voice a low and tantalizing rumble, "are the most beautiful fucking woman I've ever seen."

I turn my head, feeling a blush creep up my cheeks. "I bet you say that to all the half-naked girls you see."

"No," he rasps, his lips an inch from one of my nipples. "I don't."

When his mouth closes around me there, I arch, gasping like I've been struck by a live wire.

The thing is, normally I'd assume that men would say anything to me in this position. That they'd lie to get what they wanted.

Marco doesn't lie.

Oh sure, he withholds information. He uses his considerable intellect to his advantage.

But I've never heard him tell an outright lie…

Not like I did.

I shake off the thought. I didn't lie to Marco; I didn't tell him who I was. It wasn't relevant until it was.

His teeth bite lightly on the underside of my breast, shocking me back into the moment. I moan, my fingers scraping along the back of his neck and his well-trimmed hair.

"The things you do to me," he rumbles.

He has absolutely no idea.

"I want more. Please," I whisper. I don't even care that I'm begging.

It feels safe to beg him because I know he'll give me exactly what I want.

Marco grunts, picking me up again, spinning me over to the worn leather couch. It's warm now, from the fire that he lit before he went to shower. My back sticks slightly to the leather, but Marco's hands on my hips distract me. He tugs my pants down, leaving me bare to the fire.

And to him.

It's so much like that time at the cottage…

The night that he found out about me.

I shudder. I don't want history to repeat itself, but I'm not sure at this point what Marco knows and doesn't know about me.

And I don't want to ruin this moment. Not when I want it so badly.

Not when I need him like I need my next breath.

Marco's eyes are so dark, they look black. I can see the fire reflected there, and when he looks at me, with the flickering light caressing his skin, he looks like some kind of primal god.

Like something from a fairy tale.

"I'm going to taste you," he rumbles. One of his big hands slides up my leg, pushing it to the side, opening me to him.

I throw my head back, arching my chest up. He groans, and one hand presses against my hip, pinning me to the couch.

I'm halfway to telling him that he's being bossy and arrogant and that I need him to hurry up when he takes one long lick at my center.

All the words fly from my mind after that.

There's nothing left to do except *feel*. Every sensation feels like a revelation. I somehow notice everything... the way Marco plays with the center of my pleasure. The grip of his hands on my thighs. The way one of his hands slowly escapes and moves up to grab my breast, as though it has a mind of its own.

The way his tongue spears inside me, then retreats.

The way he consumes me like a starving man, and I can do nothing but hold on.

"God, Roisin. Your taste. It's everything I've ever fucking wanted," he groans.

I should probably warn him that I've never actually come before like this. I'd also like the chance to taste him as well, while we're on the subject...

I wiggle a little, trying to escape his grasp, but his hands push down on me hard enough that I crack an eye open to look at him.

The look he gives me is wicked. There's no other word to describe it.

"Where do you think you're going?" he growls.

"I...well, you see, I've just never... this is not going to um... work," I say, well aware of how lame my words sound. I don't want to tell him that I haven't had a partner before. I have no idea if he can make me come like this, but I definitely don't want to give the impression that I don't know what he's doing.

That he's the only one to touch me like this.

Marco pulls back. His lips shine with my moisture, and the sight makes me blush.

"You've never come like this, right?"

I shake my head from side to side, embarrassment choking any chance of words off.

"And you think that's going to stop me from trying?"

My jaw works, opening and shutting. How do I tell him that I'm nervous? That I don't want him to feel like a failure? That I don't want to disappoint him when he can't make me finish this way?

Marco chuckles, the sound vibrating the whole way up into my center. "Oh Roisin. Have you ever seen me turn down a challenge before?"

"Wait..." I protest weakly.

But it's too late.

His lips return, his tongue working me with a kind of intensity and precision that makes me jackknife up off the couch. I wriggle again, but he tugs me closer.

Marco looks up at me, the challenge clear in his gaze.

When he presses one thick finger inside me, I lean back, gasping at the pressure.

He laughs. "Oh I think you can do better than that, Roisin."

Another finger joins the first.

The pressure is intense. It's exquisite. Somehow he works a spot deep inside my body that makes me feel like I'm about to fall apart at the seams. When a third finger is added, I writhe, part in pleasure, part in pain.

But not bad pain. The type of pain that seems to scrape each of my nerves, one by one, until I'm just putty in Marco's hands.

It's somewhere in this boneless state that I notice something building at the base of my awareness, at the edge of my spine. I've had orgasms before; I'm not unfamiliar with the sensation.

But the way this one feels is entirely different.

"I can feel you, Roisin," Marco grunts from between my legs. "I need you to come for me, baby."

"Marco..."

"Come for me," he commands.

God help me.

His words push me over the edge.

I scream, my hands scrambling for purchase on the couch, tugging at his hair as I try to get away from him, try to get closer to him. I'm not sure where I need to go, because the orgasm that's ripping through me robs me of all my senses.

"Good girl," he rasps.

I shudder, the words somehow sinking an extra little punch into the waves of desire already racking my body. I don't know where I end, or where Marco begins.

I don't even know if I'm fully in control of myself, or if he's the only one in charge.

Eventually, the buzzing in my head settles down. My breath rasps in and out of my lungs, and I'm aware of the loud noise it makes in the otherwise quiet cabin.

Marco waits, patiently, at the edge of the couch.

I prop myself up on my elbows, blinking down at him.

It's a good thing that his lips turn up into a smile, because I've no idea what to say.

"No one else has made you come like that?" he growls.

Numb, I nod.

"Good. Because what I want to do to you Roisin, no one will ever do. Do you hear me? The way I'm going to fuck you, there will be no other man who can do that like I can."

I want to roll my eyes, but I'm struck with another one of those stray thoughts.

Marco doesn't lie.

I gulp. Does he mean right now? As in, we're going to do this at the moment? Here? On the couch, this very second?

His eyes flash. "Do you want that?"

Of course I do. I nod.

His grin is sinful. "Good. But first, I think something is burning."

I finally notice the scent that I thought was just my own post-orgasm haze. Scrambling up, I look at the stove, and shriek. "Help me get these out!" I say.

Marco laughs, coming up to cover me with a blanket. "There's more food, love. We'll figure it out."

He moves into the kitchen, but one word rings through my mind like a bell.

Love.

18

MARCO

We end up making pasta.

It's my default, something that I learned to cook as a child, and while Roisin is tucked back in her warm clothes, watching me warily from her spot at the small dining area table, it's good to make something easy.

Something that I can focus on instead of ripping her clothes back off and taking her like an animal on the small bed.

I want her. Again. I'm going to want her forever. Even if we never did more than this, if I just had her taste in my mouth every day, it would be enough for me.

One taste of her will never be enough.

That's fucking clear as the ice dripping off the edges of the cabin walls right now.

I have no idea how to tell her. No clue what to do next.

Other than we have to figure out who the fuck is hunting her, and I'll make them regret the fucking day that they were born.

Roisin is mine. I'll move heaven and earth to protect her.

And anyone who gets in my way is going to be fucking wrecked.

"So this one's new. Why didn't you make this for me before?" she motions to the pasta, which is absolutely nothing special. Butter, cheese, noodles, and some lightly grilled chicken.

But it smells like heaven, I'll admit.

"This was Caterina's favorite," I say, the truth flowing from me far too easily. "Whenever she had a bad day as a kid, this is what she'd ask for."

"Did you make it?"

I shrug. "Sometimes. Sometimes it was the cook or my mom. But this one always reminds me of her."

Roisin takes a bite, the noodles expertly twirled on her fork. She shuts her eyes, moaning in a way that makes my blood rush right to my cock again.

Focus, De Luca.

"Caterina was a cute kid. Cute baby."

"She's five years younger than you?" Roisin asks.

I nod.

Her nose wrinkles. "That puts you at a near decade older than me."

"What can I say," I wink at her. "You're mature for your age?"

She snorts. "You can say that again, I suppose."

"I know you had to grow up too fast, Roisin. I'd change all of that if I could," I say. My voice has dropped an octave, fury deepening it.

She pauses, her green eyes searching my face. "You would, wouldn't you?"

"Do you think I wouldn't?"

Roisin shrugs. "I do think you would, Marco. That's the interesting part. Lots of people would make empty threats—"

"Not people worth their fucking salt," I rasp.

She huffs a laugh. "Even in the world we live in, people make empty threats."

"I take all threats seriously, Roisin. The ones that I make, and the ones made against me and the people I care for."

Her green eyes narrow. "And where do I stand in that?"

Something in her voice stops me from telling her exactly where she ranks.

"Eat your pasta," I smile instead, spinning some up for myself as well.

Roisin's eyebrows raise, but she does as I ask.

The fact that she's always so willing to follow my commands, despite the fact it's not in her nature to blindly follow an order, gives me a thrill.

Roisin trusts me.

I deeply want to know how much she's willing to listen to.

If I command her to crawl across the floor to me, to suck on my..."

"You know, this place is nice," she cuts off my train of thought.

I nod, looking around. "It's very secluded."

"Hence why I thought you'd try to murder me."

I laugh. "Never, Roisin."

I'd never do anything to hurt you.

"Almost secluded enough to forget about you know... everything," she waves her fork.

I can practically see her deflating.

"You weren't sold, Roisin."

She blinks at me.

"You've had a shit hand of cards. You really have. But I think your mother probably thought she was doing what's best for you."

"It's not the choice I would make for my child," she mutters fiercely.

A smile tugs at the corner of my lips. "We never talked about that, before."

"About what?" she licks the edge of her fork, and I go still at the sight of her pink tongue darting out at the edge of the metal.

"Kids," I grunt.

Roisin leans back. "Well why would we? We were only pretending to be a couple then."

The unspoken question, the one that asks *and what are we now*, lingers between us.

"Still. It might have helped with our cover. Helps with it now, actually."

"Oh pish. We're not still pretending we're a couple, are we?" Roisin rolls her eyes.

I put my elbows down on the dining room table. "I'm not pretending."

Her nose wrinkles. "Marco…"

"Kids. Tell me."

Roisin sighs. "I've never really thought about it. Obviously my own childhood was shite, and so I'm not exactly partial to repeating that on a child of my own."

"I see."

She smirks at me. "I'd imagine you're the opposite. Big family, you want to have kids like rabbits. Your own football team, yeah?"

"No," I say sharply.

A little too sharply.

Rosin huffs. "Okay well. I was just asking."

"I know," I amend. "I'm just… You know, I feel like I raised most of my siblings."

"Even Dino?"

I nod. "Even Dino. The fact that he's close in age didn't mean shit. The second they were born, I was in charge of them. They were my responsibility as much as my parents', even more so in some ways."

"So that leaves you…" her voice trails off.

I sigh. "I guess I've never thought about it either, because of that. Everything I've ever done has been to set them up for success."

"That sounds lonely."

My eyes shoot to hers. "What?"

"Lonely. I mean, you didn't even get to be a brother to them if you had to be part father, part brother, part random parent. You didn't get to have siblings. They got to, among each other, I'd imagine. But if you were constantly policing them, then you weren't a sibling, Marco."

Her words shake me, but it feels like they're shaking something loose instead of breaking me.

I think of Sal, Dino, and Caterina. I love them. No question about it. But, we're all very different people. The more that I think about it, I wonder how close we really all are.

Or, maybe they're close.

And I'm not.

I frown. Surely that can't be right. I comb through my brain, trying to think about how our dynamics play out. Dino struggled to fit in with all of us. Sal and Caterina were close, of course, but the three of them have a dynamic that I've never really been able to engage with.

"I guess you're right," I say slowly. "They are siblings to each other. And I'm not."

I've never said anything like it out loud before.

Somehow, the acute loneliness inside of me feels... soothed. It's miserable, of course, to realize that I've always thought

Dino was the one who was on the outside of our family, and to realize that it was never Dino.

It was me.

God, I'm such an asshole. I've been such an asshole to him.

I need to do something with the guilt that's swamping me.

But at least realizing the fact that I'm the one who has always been apart in our sibling dynamic, feels like the emotion that's been itching at me is no longer rattling around my chest.

Settled.

I feel settled.

Roisin leans back in her chair. She sighs, and the sight brings my blood rushing back to my cock.

Feeding her, apparently, turns me on.

Then again. There's very little that doesn't turn me on about Roisin.

I smirk at her. "Would you like me to give you more?"

The blush that heats her cheeks is worth it. "Food, you mean?" she says, coughing a little around the words.

"Sure."

Roisin rolls her eyes, her cheeks a marvelous shade of red. "Well. Why don't I help you clean up first."

"No way. Why don't you relax, and I'll clean up?"

Her eyebrow arches up. "I don't need special treatment, Marco."

"Stop. I'll treat you how I want to. And if that's cleaning up after cooking, then you don't need to do anything about it," I growl.

Roisin studies me for a second. "I'm not sure if this is bullying, or if you're trying to do something nice."

"Take it however you want," I rumble at her.

She sighs, then stretches. "Fine, I'll be here in front of the fire."

I watch her stand and slink to the leather couch. She lies down, and I fetch a blanket, covering her from head to toe.

Sleepy green eyes blink up at me. "Marco…"

"Relax," I urge.

I turn, smiling lightly.

Roisin is mine. Caring for her is a kink I hadn't known that I even had.

Until now.

By the time the dishes are done, she's sound asleep.

I consider taking her into the bedroom, but the glow of the fire on her curly hair is so fucking pretty, I decide that it's easier to leave her there. I drag a dining room chair over so I'm sort of next to her, looking at the fire, and I pull out my phone.

Turning it on, the first thing I do is make sure I'm connected to the secure satellite service that I pay an arm and a leg for. No need to alert anyone to our location.

Next, I check the cameras at the lake house.

The frame loads slowly, but when it finishes, my heart leaps and my blood boils.

The house is fucking *trashed*.

I zoom in, pivoting the functioning security cameras around. It looks like someone broke in through the front door, which is fully off its hinges. Shit is scattered everywhere; it looks like someone just overturned everything trying to search the house.

I frown.

What the hell were they even looking for?

The wreckage doesn't look like people who were searching for a person. It looks almost like someone just looking for a document, or some kind of item.

Or money, I guess.

It could also be that there's something I'm missing. Maybe the point of all the carnage is just to scare Roisin. It makes no sense, though... why would they bother, when they know that she's with me?

A text comes through. Liam. I open it, frowning at the words.

Liam: Tell Roisin that she needs to publicly take a role in the family if she wants this to stop. Don't know what's going on, but I can't protect her if she's still trying to play both sides of the field.

I growl.

Me: I'll let her do what she wants to do.

Liam: Do it, DeLuca.

Me: This is probably your fault. Look for your own enemies.

Liam: It's not me.

That gives me pause.

What the hell would he be talking about?

At that moment, Elio calls. I stand, quickly moving to the edge of the bathroom, quietly closing the door so I don't wake Roisin. "What?" I hiss.

"Dino saw a ghost today."

I roll my eyes. "The fuck does that mean?"

"I mean, he saw someone who shouldn't be alive."

My body stiffens. "Who?"

Elio sighs. "He doesn't know. But his cousin, Nico? Swears it was his uncle."

"Dino's uncle, or Nico's?"

"Nico's."

The implication rings through me like a bullet.

"No," I whisper.

Dino's father should be dead. End of story. There's no way that he's alive; not after my father and all of his rivals came for him.

"He's dead."

"Nico's father is dead. The man he saw looked just like him. An identical twin," Elio mutters.

"That can't possibly be."

"Check your sources. If he comes for Dino…"

"He wont. The Drakos family has fully embraced Dino and Marisol," I say quickly. It helps that Marisol brought a vast criminal empire spanning the entirety of South America to the marriage, elevating the previously defunct Drakos family name to one that's whispered with real fear now.

"Maybe," Elio says slowly. "But then, what else would he want?"

My mind churns.

"Revenge?"

"That's what I thought," Elio repeats grimly. "I've put everyone in Italy on high alert, and sent additional support to Greece."

"They can look after themselves," I mutter. The ransacked lake house, which is attached only to me, is weighing heavily on my mind.

Moretti, though, wanted to kidnap the girls.

And then the attack on Liam...

Could this be multiple different people?

"Marco," Elio barks.

"What?"

"Tell me what you're thinking."

I hesitate.

It's not that I don't want to tell Elio what's going on. I could need his help, and knowing that he's one of the closest people I have to handle this makes me want to.

But I...

"I know, you don't want to. I know. But what trouble are you in?"

I open the bathroom door and look at Roisin. "It's not me," I say, closing the door.

Elio sucks in a breath.

"I can't tell you everything. But I think... I think that I need to protect someone. And I think that she might be in danger because of me."

The puzzle pieces are clicking into place. When I was in witness protection, I left, several times, to confirm that Dino was a son of the Drakos family. I gave him the information, and I connected him to his cousin, Nico, in order to help him and Marisol.

And then I went home, every night, to Roisin. In our little cottage, where we played the perfect couple.

"Marco..."

"Is it still the case that wives are off limits?" I ask suddenly.

I can practically feel Elio's frown. "I would not say always, but among those who play by the laws, yes."

"Thanks."

"Marco, do not do what I think you're going to do."

"Thank you, Elio. I'll call if I need you."

I hang up the phone before he can answer.

Opening the bathroom door, I creep to the couch. If Roisin has been under threat this whole time because of our association, then there's only one solution.

I need to make sure that in the eyes of our community, she's untouchable. Because if she's harmed and she's my wife, then whoever is after her will face the consequences not just from me...

But from the entire community.

Fuck.

I put a hand on Roisin's shoulder. Gently, I shake her.

She blinks, her eyes focusing on me slowly. "Marco? Is everything okay?"

I take a deep breath.

"We need to get married."

19

ROISIN

I cannot possibly have heard him right.

I sit up on the couch, trying to blink the sleep from my eyes. "Marco. What did you just say?"

"We need to get married," he repeats, his brown eyes staring at me like I'm the one who's said something utterly insane.

I shake my head. "No."

"Yes."

"No, Marco."

"Yes, we do."

Anger lights me like a match. "Well you can't just tell me that! You're not even going to ask?"

He tilts his head. "Sorry. Let me explain."

After a five minute long word vomit that's unfortunately extremely easy for me to follow, I'm still just as shocked.

"Let me make sure that I'm understanding you correctly. You think that there's separate people who are after you... and I. And that one of those people is the father of your brother, Dino. The father who is supposed to be very, very dead. Who was killed, in fact, by your father."

He nods.

"And you think that this person is trying to attack me, because he thinks that we're like... together."

Marco nods again.

"And somehow, getting more together, meaning being married, would prevent this?"

"Not from him," Marco says quickly.

I tilt my head, confusion clouding my face.

"Let's say that the French, for example, hear that Dino's father is coming for the wife of Marco De Luca. This is not done, and while my alliance with the French is tentative at best, it might give them an excuse to air an old grievance or do something to fucking gain the support of the De Lucas," he explains.

My head feels like it's spinning.

"It's politics, mostly. People know that I'm attached to Elio, and they know our families are powerful. They might be willing to hop in and support us, if they knew you are part of the family."

I'm staring at him.

"So it's not really marriage," I say slowly. "It's a bargain."

I can't help the hurt that laces through my words.

Marco's eyes widen. "No, it's not that, Roisin. It's..."

"It's a bargain," I say flatly. "It's something that you're thinking will keep me safe, but not because you want me."

Marco's eyes darken. "Roisin..."

"I'm going to take a shower," I announce.

I don't really need, or want, to shower. It's just the only place in this tiny cabin that I can get away from him.

I turn on the shower, taking off my clothes. I let the steam fill the small room, then step inside. The water is blissfully hot, and scalds my skin as I let it pound into me.

I feel like screaming.

Why doesn't anyone actually want me?

Why am I just some kind of bargaining piece?

Why...

I don't make it to the next thought. In between breaths, which are coming very quickly because I'm trying not to cry, a naked Marco appears in the shower with me.

Before I have time to scream at him to get out, he leans in and kisses me.

And I lose all coherent thought.

Marco's kisses are addicting. I know this. But this one is much more. It feels like fire on my skin, and I can't think straight around it. He's everywhere; his hands on my face, in my hair, tugging my mouth up to meet him. I moan, lost in the moment as he rubs his considerable length against me.

Marco pulls back, his eyes fierce. His pupils are blown so wide that they're almost totally black.

"I want you more than life itself," he growls.

The words lodge in my mind, somewhere, but I don't have any time to register them.

Marco's tongue opens my mouth, and I gasp as he takes me in the most breathtakingly dominant kiss I've ever experienced.

I have no choice. I have no agency. There's nothing I can do to resist him or escape him.

All I can do is submit.

I don't want to anyway. The way that Marco's been caring for me has melted my heart to the point where I'm kind of concerned that I won't be able to recover.

I guess it's just another element of the storm that is Marco De Luca.

He spins me around so I'm facing the shower tiles. Pressing me forward, I gasp as my nipples graze against the cool surface. It makes me arch my back instinctively, and Marco meets me when I do, his tongue licking a long line up from my collarbone to my ear. Standing behind me he's like a furnace, and I tilt my hips back, my ass grazing against his hard length as I do.

He grunts. "Don't move," he groans.

I freeze.

"I want this to last," Marco manages to grit out.

I don't think I do.

His teeth graze my neck and I moan, my nerves a wreck as I think about what it would feel like for him to bite…

Ah.

I want to scream, but instead I let out a little gasping breath as his teeth pinch down, gently but firmly, on the tendon in my neck.

Shit, this should not feel this good...

But it does.

I moan as he lifts off of me, wanting that pressure again. Marco's hands roam my body. One grips the back of my neck, pulling me slightly off of the cold tiles, while the other traces a line between my ass cheeks and pushes my legs apart.

"You're so fucking hot," Marco growls in my ear.

I moan as he presses a thick finger inside of me.

"You're so eager, Roisin. So needy. You want me to fuck you, to drive into your hot little pussy, don't you?"

Good Lord.

My eyes practically roll back in my head. Marco's always been good with his words, but this is more than just that.

This is like pure fire, traveling from my ears to my core.

I practically melt, grateful that his arm is holding me up, because otherwise I'd be a mess all over the tiny bathroom right now.

Marco spears into me, and I groan and shudder as he thrusts his fingers inside me. "I'm going to fuck you senseless, Roisin," he grunts. "You're going to come all over my cock, and you're going to fucking scream my name while you do it."

I dare you, I want to say.

Instead, I just moan.

Marco laughs, a low noise that makes me shudder closer to an orgasm. I'd be shocked that I'm this close, but with Marco…

I'm not.

He pulls his fingers from me seconds before the shake of the orgasm takes me, and I practically whimper as he does. Gently, he turns me in his arms, then his hands drift down my sides and grab the sides of my ass.

"Wrap your legs around me, love," he whispers.

I would do anything he asked me to right now.

Marco hoists me up in a smooth movement, and I slide down his stomach, marveling at the abs that ripple under my hot center. He pauses me, his firm grip balancing me with ease.

His eyes are so dark. "Wrap your hands around me and push me inside your sweet pussy, Roisin."

I take one arm from his neck and grip him, shocked at how hard and smooth his cock is. Marco makes a groaning noise, and for one devilish second, I think about disobeying him.

His eyes flash. "Don't you fucking dare," he barks. "I'm going to watch you take every drop of my come, Roisin. Don't you fucking dare think of anything else."

Well.

I notch him at my entrance. My hand drifts back up to hold on to his strong neck, and slowly, he lowers me onto the length of his cock.

At first, there's a stretch. He's so huge; it would be hard to not feel every inch of him. I'm determined to keep a straight face so he doesn't know I've never done this before.

But then he seems to go on.

And on.

And on.

I'm panting, practically writhing with the fullness, when finally I feel his hips bump against me. My legs wrap tightly around his hips and I hold on to his neck, clinging to him.

Impaled by him.

"You're such a good girl, Roisin," he croons in my ear. "Look how fucking well you take me. Look how I fit around you, my perfect girl."

Jesus Christ. I never knew how bad of a praise kink I had until this precise moment.

"Marco," I whisper.

I don't know what else to do. What else to say.

Slowly, he starts to move.

It's a little awkward at first. Marco and I scramble to find a rhythm, but once he starts to move my hips up and down, bouncing me over his thick cock, I finally figure it out. All the while, Marco whispers in my ear. He's not saying anything particularly. He tells me that I'm a good girl, that I take him well, that my pussy fits him and only him.

I'm inclined to agree.

Especially because I have nothing to compare it to.

My legs are shaking, my arms feel like they're going to melt, but Marco keeps moving me, the pace relentless and steady. I breathe, my eyes slowly shutting, lost in the rhythm of our bodies.

I'm almost lulled into a dreamy state…

And then the orgasm shatters my world.

I scream. I scream his name. I scream obscenities and words that I'm not even sure I really knew I had. Marco follows me, I think, because I'm vaguely aware of the fact that his movements have gone from smooth and calculated to rapid and jagged, and then he shouts my name as he comes.

I swear I can feel him come. I swear, there's a jet of heat and a pulsing inside me that has nothing to do with the shower...

Especially because the shower is getting quite cold.

I shiver, Marco still inside me. His eyes go wide. "Fuck," he mutters. "You're cold."

"I'm fine," I say.

But I can't stop the goosebumps that chase over my skin.

Marco doesn't bother to shut the shower off. He storms from the room, both of us dripping. Gently, he deposits me on the floor in front of the fire. "Stay here," he mutters.

I shiver, the fire warming my skin as I watch him retreat and return with two oversized fluffy towels.

I reach for one, but Marco shakes his head. "Let me," he whispers.

Silently, I nod.

Marco tucks the towel around me with practiced movements, before taking the other one to my hair. He's still naked, dripping onto the wood floor of the cabin, and I trace the path of water on his skin as it gleams in the firelight.

I probably shouldn't look at his cock again.

But when I do, I'm surprised to find it half-hard.

He chuckles. "You have quite an impact on me, Roisin."

"What do you mean?"

"I'm always like this for you," he murmurs.

My eyes fly to his, and I see absolutely no signs of a lie there.

Eventually he gets himself a towel, wrapping all that luscious skin away. Marco sighs, glancing over me like he's looking for something.

"Are you dry enough?" he asks, his voice concerned. "I could get another towel..."

"I'm fine. Tired," I whisper.

He nods. I squeak as he leans in and literally whisks me off my feet, then laugh as he tucks me into the bed. I wiggle. "Wet towel and all?"

"Take them off," he rumbles.

His eyes go dark as I take off the towel and hand it to him, clutching the sheets to my chest like I'm some kind of blushing virgin.

Marco disappears putting the towels away, then slides into the bed with me. I sigh as he pulls me close, an arm tugging me against his middle.

"You're like a damn furnace," I murmur as he warms my back.

"It works, I guess, since you're like an icicle half the time."

I don't have a response to that.

We lay quietly, listening to the fire as it crackles and pops. I watch the light from the flames dance against the far wall, my mind whirling.

I don't know what to do with this.

His question feels like it's hanging over my head. Married? I see the logic, but I'm not sure I want to follow it. My mother, after all, fell for something similar with my father.

Would I just be falling for something with Marco?

Falling, of course, being an objective word. I've already fallen, to some extent.

My heart feels like it's going to explode, and there's no doubt that I'm in love with Marco De Luca. But I also don't want to just be another tool, another thing that people use or keep in order to further their own goals.

He said it was for my protection though...

"Roisin?" Marco murmurs.

The sleepy sound of his voice cuts right through me, and I feel like I'm aching to tell him how I feel.

"Yes?" I murmur. I can't turn around and look at him. If I do, I'm going to melt.

"We need to get married," he whispers.

I take a deep breath. I shut my eyes.

"Okay."

20

MARCO

One good thing about Europe: it never takes long to find a priest.

And certainly never takes long to find one that's willing to take a bribe.

The whole thing takes probably an hour, maybe two, to arrange. I'm not quite ready to tell Elio yet, so I call around, working my contacts until I find a space that will take us on short notice. It's expensive, sure, but with the amount of buildings that need to be preserved and the waning state of Catholicism in Europe, once money's on the table, the priest agrees to meet us in an hour.

The sun is just breaking over the tops of the mountains when I bundle her into the car, our bags already there.

The road rolls away underneath the tires, and I feel like I need to do something. Say something. But every time I open my mouth to ask more than a surface-level question, nothing comes out.

I have truly no idea what to say to her.

Far too quickly, we arrive at the destination. I peer over the dashboard, squinting at the tiny building in front of us, nestled in a small alpine valley that would be picturesque if we weren't here to get married and get on out of here.

It's nice. The building is tiny. I snort.

Roisin and I are going to be married in a chapel that's somewhere around a billion years old. I don't know, actually, and I don't care, because as we sit and stare at it, I'm not thinking of the stones around us.

I'm only thinking of her.

She hasn't said much since we left the cabin. Just kind of perfunctory stuff. This morning when she got dressed, she put on the only dress in the bags that I packed for her. It's a sundress, a light green color that looks nice with her hair and her skin, with a flared skirt and a tighter bodice that pushes up her breasts.

Distracted, I don't notice that her hands are shaking until we're almost at the door of the little chapel.

I pause. "Are you okay?" I ask. She might be fucking cold. I mean of course she is. I'm an idiot. It's fucking winter up here. The wind is still icy, and I hastily shrug off my coat and put it on her shoulders.

There, that should do it.

Roisin gives me a tight smile. "Fine."

Pointedly, I look down at her hands, because they're still shaking like crazy.

Clearly she notices my stare. With some hesitation, she curls her fingers under her palms. "Well they don't exactly say that having a wedding day is a walk in the park," she mutters defensively.

Fuck. Of course this is about the whole wedding thing. Clearly, she's been thinking about it all morning, and I was too focused to tell. "They say that, but they also say everyone gets cold feet on their wedding day."

"Yeah," she offers lamely.

I can tell she's trying to walk it off, but I'm not sure why. She agreed to this. She said it was a good idea. I suck in a breath. "Roisin..."

"I'm fine, Marco. I just... she huffs."

I pause.

Roisin's eyes look down. "Look, it's just a lot. It's rushed. And that's not a bad thing, it's just... different. I don't even have flowers or anything."

Fuck.

I know I saw something, which felt impossible because there's literally snow on the ground. While spring might be touching the other areas of the world, here in the Italian Alps, there's still snow everywhere.

Tracing back our steps, I see them. There. Impossibly small flowers that are pushing up under the crust of snow in a sunny area.

"Probably some kind of fucking protected flower," I mutter. It is on the grounds of this monastery that feels ancient, so it's entirely possible.

Still, I reach beneath the crust of the snow and pull up enough to be a small handful.

I hop back across the snow, my feet fucking freezing because of the moisture from the snow. I hand Roisin the flowers. "Here," I mutter.

She blinks. "How did you..."

"Saw them on the way in."

"Snowdrops," she murmurs.

Her hand touches mine as she pulls the little clutch of flowers to her chest.

I raise my eyebrow. "Is that what they're called?"

"Yeah. They're the first things that bloom in the winter. Up here, anyway. We don't have them in Ireland, since it doesn't snow there quite as often, but yeah. Snowdrops."

"Well. Snowdrops. That's what they are," I say, watching to see Roisin's reaction.

Her shoulders relax, slightly.

It's not quite the reaction that I'm hoping for. I want her to be okay. I want her to feel good about this, about *us*.

But she doesn't.

This is to protect her.

It's a silent reminder of what's important to remember right now, but looking at Roisin's face, it doesn't help me feel any better.

I did this to her.

I'm the one who decided that we needed to get married.

So you can keep her safe.

Unfortunately, I don't think I'm keeping her safe right now. Right now, it looks like I'm the only one causing her pain.

Guilt floods me.

"Roisin…"

"Let's just get this over with, yeah?" she says. I watch as her eyes seem to shutter, and she looks at the door to the chapel.

I want to stop her. Hold her hand. Keep her back with me.

But as soon as I reach for her, she's already pushing the door open and walking inside.

I clench my fist, pulling it tightly against my thigh.

Let's just get this over with.

I don't want to be something that Roisin "gets over with".

The circumstances aren't ideal, sure.

But as I watch her move into the chapel, greeting the truly ancient looking man inside, I can't help but feel a deep, unsettling feeling. I'm enraged, with myself.

Why not me? Why doesn't Roisin want to marry me?

Upset, I follow her into the church.

Roisin doesn't want me. I'm forcing her into this.

Maybe the only protection she needs isn't from anyone…

Except me.

The whole ceremony takes less than thirty minutes.

Probably.

I'm sweating bullets, and it's the longest thirty minutes of my life. All I can think about is Roisin.

Is she happy? Is she okay? I want to look over at her, but the priest keeps droning on and on in Italian, and I know I'm not supposed to look over at her...

Finally, the priest wraps up. He stares at the two of us, and then says in Italian, "You can kiss your bride, young man."

I freeze.

Roisin looks up at me. "What'd he say?"

"He... we're done," I grunt.

The priest gives me an eyebrow raise, but I quickly grab Roisin's hand. "We're done," I grunt.

She makes a noise, but follows me out of the little chapel.

I tug her over the stones and shove her back into the car. I can't help it; I feel like a fucking caveman right now. I overwhelmingly want to bring Roisin back to a house and fuck her senseless.

I start up the car, the Land Rover roaring to life as I practically burn the tires screaming out of the small gravel parking lot.

"What the hell was that?" Roisin says, barking at me.

"He was being creepy."

"What did he say?"

I squeeze the wheel. "He told me to kiss you."

Roisin's jaw drops. "Like, as in kiss the bride? The totally normal, regular thing that people say to newlyweds basically every single time?"

The leather of the car steering wheel squeaks under my fingers as I grind down on it.

"You're kidding, Marco. Seriously? That's what he said?"

"He was a fucking creep."

She rolls her eyes. "Jaysus Christ, Marco—"

I jerk the wheel of the car, making Roisin squeak. There's not a lot of space on these tiny mountain roads, but I manage to pull over into a little space tucked up against the side of the rocky face, the gravel spraying from under our tires as I do.

Roisin screeches. "What in the—"

I cut her off, my lips covering hers as I silence her.

The kiss isn't soft, and it isn't easy. It's full of all my frustration, and the confusion, and the deep anguish I feel every time I think about what I've done to Roisin. What I've brought on her.

What I've fucked up, and I'm now worried I can't ever fix.

What I want.

I know it's not right. She might not want this. Hell, I probably just ruined her whole life.

But I don't fucking care.

Under my lips, she's stiff, and I hate it. I hate that she might hate me.

When I want her so damn badly, I can't fucking stand it.

I scoot my hand around to the back of her neck, gripping her tightly, twining her beautiful hair in my fingers as I tug gently. Roisin gasps, and I take the opportunity to explore her mouth.

I'm so fucking sorry.

I want you so fucking bad...

She moans, and my world lights on fire.

Roisin kissing me back changes everything. The hunger roaring inside me softens, turning into something less violent.

But no less hungry.

Her fingers trace the outline of my jaw, trailing down my chest. I love how strong she is, how capable and tough she is.

And even though I know it's completely illogical, all I want to do is protect her from every fucking asshole with a gun that wants to hurt her.

I break the kiss, moving along the side of her face, kissing and licking until I find the place where her neck meets her shoulders. I bite, gently, rewarded by a little moan from her that makes me go harder than the fucking granite around us.

"Marco..."

Something loud screams by. A truck, a bus, I don't fucking know.

It's enough to snap me out of my frenzied state.

I lean back, panting, staring at Roisin. Her eyes are wide, and I can see a red mark forming at her neck.

It gives me an insane amount of satisfaction to know that I marked her.

She parts her lips, swollen red from our kiss. "Why?"

"Why what?" I growl.

"You didn't want to kiss me in the church."

The worry in her eyes makes my stomach churn, but I put my hand up, gently cupping the side of her cheek.

Warily, she looks at me before leaning into my hand for just a fraction of a second.

"Every time I kiss you, Roisin, I don't want to stop," I whisper. The truth feels painful to let go, but her eyes snapping to mine encourage me to keep going.

I gently run my thumb over her lips.

"Every time I kiss you, I want more. I want to fuck you senseless, until you're screaming my name, and every fucking time it's not the right time," I practically growl.

Her cheeks flush red, and I'm reminded that when she blushes, it spreads down her neck in a very, very sexy way.

"So no," I grit out. "I didn't want that old fucking man there. I don't want to kiss you in a car on the side of the road, or in a hot spring. I want you where I can have you, and until you name the time and place, I can't fucking kiss you like I want to. Because if I do, I won't ever be able to stop."

I drop my hand, the truth hanging uncomfortably in the car. I pull back out, following the road as we drive back toward the little cabin that I rented.

Roisin hasn't said anything. Part of me paces like a fucking dog in a cage, worried that I said too much.

Most of me though?

Is relieved.

The truth is out there. She has it now.

And I don't want to take it back.

21

ROISIN

UNTIL YOU NAME THE TIME AND PLACE.

I THOUGHT THAT IF I WAS SOMEONE'S WIFE, THE circumstances would be wildly different. For example, I had thought that my mother, at the very least, would be there. Probably not my father, certainly, but my mother at least.

I had also imagined once, long ago, that my husband and I would be wildly in love.

A fantasy, to be sure, but not an unreasonable one.

What I had never imagined was that I would be sitting, alone, in a Range Rover in the Italian Alps while my new husband investigates to make sure our latest mountain hideout was safe.

And I had certainly never thought that I would be contemplating whether or not we'd be having sex on our wedding night.

After we got back to the little cabin, Marco decided it was time to move again. He didn't say why, and I didn't ask. He drove us up the road a ways to a little town, asking around for a place for us to stay. There was, it turned out, a local place that served as an inn, which is where we currently are, with him inside ensuring that there's no reason to bounce to the next town.

I'd call him paranoid but honestly...

I approve.

The sooner we can figure out who is after me, the better, and unfortunately, we're no closer to that.

The only thing we're even remotely 'close' to, I suppose, is being man and wife.

And that brings me right back here.

To wondering what the hell I'm doing.

The kiss from earlier feels like it's still burning my lips. Really, every kiss with Marco is dangerous. It feels to me like... I'm hiking up one of these damn mountains, and someone gave me a shove. I manage to get my footing every now and then, but then another kiss with Marco, another touch from him, another moment where our bodies are drawn toward each other...

And I'm tumbling down again.

Until you name the time and place...

God above, I want him so badly it hurts.

I would be lying if I said that in my wildest, deepest, darkest fantasies, I hadn't thought about Marco as my husband.

But now that he is...

I don't know what to do with myself.

The car door opens, startling me. I look up, and Marco is standing in front of me, blocking the cold.

"We're good," he says, in that rough tone that sets my nerves on absolute haywire.

The inn, I know, is what he's talking about. He means that the inn is safe and he doesn't have any concerns.

But God.

I wish he were talking about us.

Until you name the time and place...

I shut my eyes and step out of the vehicle. I don't say anything to him. I don't trust myself to.

Because if I open my mouth?

I might just name that time and place.

The inn is quaint. A very joyful looking woman greeted us in Italian at the door, and Marco responded. I had to pretend, of course, that the sound of him murmuring sweet nothings in Italian didn't set my skin on fire, and when we arrived in the room I didn't even look around. I headed promptly to the shower.

And I locked the door.

The hot water, blissfully hot despite the weak water flow, cascades over me. Despite my efforts, I can't seem to scrub Marco's lips off of me.

Or the words that are beating a tattoo into my brain.

I change into the silk pajamas that Marco left for me, then cautiously open the door. He's sitting, stretched out on the bed, and it's only then that my brain registers the fact that there is a bed.

One.

Single.

Bed.

Tonight… I think it might be too much for me.

He's frowning, looking at his phone, and in the warm (if dim) light from the one sad bulb under the vintage lampshade, the lines between his eyebrows seem to be etched in marble.

I just want to smooth them away.

He looks up, and his brown eyes trace the outline of my body in a way that makes my nipples stand straight up. I know he notices when his eyes hitch on my chest.

I want to shrink back but…

Instead, I straighten.

"Shower's open," I murmur, my voice hoarse.

Marco tilts his head. "Roisin," he murmurs.

It's my name. One word. Two syllables.

But somehow it almost undoes me.

"What's wrong?"

I should lie to him, I know.

Instead, I drift over to the little chair that's positioned next to the bed. I tuck myself into it, sinking into the plush seat, my feet curling against the cushion. Knees to my chest, I wrap my arms around my shins and tilt my head so I'm not looking at him, but toward the door.

"This just isn't how I imagined it," I finally whisper.

I can't look at him. I hear him shift on the bed, though, and I do my best to keep my eyes trained on the door.

"I know we needed to do this, Marco. I do. And I know you're doing what you think is best to protect me. But I just... I really thought I'd be married and it would be... it wouldn't be..."

I stop before the tears scratching my throat come out.

My eyes slam shut so that I don't cry.

"Roisin," Marco's voice murmurs.

It's close.

I crack an eye open and slam it shut again.

He's kneeling on the floor.

The image of him, however, kneeling in front of me, will stick with me for the rest of my life.

"I'm so fucking sorry," he whispers.

His voice is hoarse.

I shift, looking at him fully.

"I'm sorry that we did this. If you want it to be annulled—"

"No," I cut him off.

His jaw slams shut, and I can see a muscle work underneath his bronze skin.

I must be insane. I must be absolutely losing my mind, or maybe there's some kind of ghost in here that's possessing me, because when I open my mouth, I am completely not in control of what I'm about to say.

"What if... we pretended instead."

Marco's eyes blink, and I can see confusion cross his features. "Pretend?"

I nod. I gulp, trying to fight against the fluttering of my pulse in my throat. "What if we pretend that this isn't fake. That it's real. That we're married and it's... how it should be," I whisper.

Marco De Luca is a tough man to shock.

But shock is written across every one of his features right now.

"What..."

"Pretend that I'm your wife. That this is our first night together as... married..." I murmur. "That we chose this. That we're—"

I can't say the next part.

That we're in love.

I don't think I need to say it, though

Marco's eyes look at me with so much longing, I know he knows what I'm thinking.

"Roisin..."

"I know it's not real. I know it's not," I murmur. "But just pretend... because this is the time, and this is the place."

I peek at him from under my lashes.

The longing I saw there earlier? It's been transformed.

And pure, raw lust spreads across his features.

"Do you know what you're asking me for?" he growls.

I nod.

I can't do much more than that.

Marco *moves*.

In one swift motion I'm in his arms, then another I'm being dropped onto the surprisingly comfortable bed. I want to giggle, or squeak, or just react somehow because I'm overwhelmed by too many thoughts all at once and if I don't do something, I'm going to explode.

But then Marco's lips are on mine. His big body covers me.

And I don't have time to think, or do anything other than just *feel*.

Every time before, we've been so desperate. Quick. It's been frenzied, like a fire that neither of us has any control over.

Now though?

It's almost like time is slowing. Marco kisses me in a way that's almost leisurely, like he's taking his time with me.

Like we have all the time in the world…

Fuck.

Because if we were newlyweds, we would.

It feels like a dagger in my heart, realizing that he's taking my request to pretend so seriously.

But if he can pretend… so can I.

Arching my back upwards, I murmur, "You've been waiting for so long. Through the whole ceremony."

Marco freezes, like he's trying to figure out what I'm saying.

I look up at him, where his hands are positioned on my stomach, gently tugging up the white silk pajama top.

Then, he seems to register my words. Part of the light in his eyes seems to dim.

Come on, Marco. Pretend.

I don't know if he can hear my silent words or not, but he seems to figure it out.

"My family was so annoying," he says roughly.

Okay then. I'm somewhat relieved that he's going to play along. "They're just happy for you."

"They can be happy for me without being in my business," he rumbles.

I laugh, and it's not fake. It feels so... normal.

Then, Marco's tongue traces my belly button, and I moan.

"Take this off," he groans, tugging my shirt.

I pull the silk up and over my head. It whispers to the floor, and his fingers hook in the pajama bottoms, making quick work of them. Naked before him on the bed, I want to shy away...

But that's not how I would want this to go.

If it were real.

"We should invite them over soon," I murmur.

Marco looks at me, his eyes dark, pupils blown out to the edges of his eyes. "I don't want to talk about my fucking family right now," he rasps.

I do laugh then.

Then, when his mouth latches onto my breast, I scream.

He knows how to work me. I'm not sure how he knows. But every motion seems perfectly tuned to me. His fingers press inside me, curling into a spot that makes every single part of my body shake with pleasure. His mouth bites, licks, and nibbles at my skin, like he's determining precisely where to drive me insane.

I don't know how, but Marco plays me like he knows exactly how, and within minutes an orgasm rips over me.

I'm still rocked by it when Marco kneels, pushing my legs apart.

Somehow he's shed his clothes, and I sit up slightly on my elbows...

When I see him, his body caressed in the warm light, I can't help but sigh.

He smirks, noticing my interest. I watch as his hand travels down, before he palms his rather considerable erection.

"It's all for you, Roisin," he rumbles.

He's just pretending.

"Good," I purr, leaning back. "Because you'll never have anyone else."

The words seem to hit him physically, because his cock twitches in his hand.

Within seconds, he's positioned at my entrance. I feel him there, then gasp.

"Fuck, Roisin," he murmurs. "You're so fucking tight."

"All for you," I whisper.

His eyes roll back in his head.

When Marco enters me fully, I half expect him to return to that feverish pace we had in the car.

He surprises me again, though, when he begins to move in long, full strokes.

He's thick. Every pulse makes me shudder, the echoes of my previous orgasm rippling again. I'm almost there when Marco stops, looking down at me.

"Not like this," he whispers.

He moves us, without pulling out, so that he's sitting upright and I'm straddling his lap. From this position, we can look each other in the eyes.

I go to look away, but Marco pulls my face to his.

"I want to see you, darling."

Darling.

I know it's fake.

But when we start to move, almost as one, I can almost believe it.

My eyes are locked on Marco's. My breathing changes, until I see myself breathe in line with his chest as it rises and falls.

One of his hands drifts down to my clit, and I shudder as he touches me.

"Come with me, Roisin," he grunts.

I can't resist.

His thumb touches me once, and I shatter.

I gasp, falling forward onto Marco's strong shoulders. He jerks, pulsing up into me, and I can feel him inside me as he tucks me tightly against him.

I can feel his heart beating in his chest...

And I can feel my own heart echoing his.

We sit like that, for what feels like an eternity, until I shiver.

Gently, Marco untangles us. He cleans me up with a towel from the bathroom, and then tucks me into the sheets next to him.

I'm drowsy, but more than that, I don't know what to do with myself, so I shut my eyes and even my breathing.

That was the most intimate sex I've ever had. And it's all fake.

Because Marco and I were just pretending.

I can't even pretend that my heart isn't aching right now. There's nothing more in the world that I want right now than to be Marco's wife for real. Than to have him love me, fully, and have all of this be *real*.

But it's not.

My heart feels like it's skipping every fourth beat, and my head is swirling. I'm doing my best to make it seem like I'm asleep, but inside, I feel like I'm being torn apart.

Marco stirs. "Roisin?"

I don't answer. *I'm asleep.*

He waits a second, then I feel him press a kiss to my shoulder.

"I'm not pretending," he whispers.

Thank God he thinks I'm asleep.

Because if I had to face that?

I'm not sure what I would do.

22

MARCO

Waking up with Roisin in my arms, I know beyond a shadow of a doubt that I love this woman.

And I need to divorce her as soon as possible.

What Roisin and I did last night wasn't okay.

And that makes it dangerous, not only for her, but for me.

I'm not built to have a wife. Not like my brothers and sister. I'm not like them.

My role is to make sure everyone is safe. That they have the lives they want, that they're happy and fulfilled.

And Roisin isn't safe if she's attached to me.

Because I've already fucked it up for her. I've already taken away her option to choose everything she wants.

Clearly.

She hates me. I know she does. She was only able to have sex with me like we did if she was pretending, and that hurts like hell.

I hate myself for taking the chance when I saw it.

When she told me she wanted me to pretend, it fucking killed me.

But I did it anyway.

I waited until she fell asleep to tell her that it wasn't pretend for me. That it was real.

That everything we did, was something I wanted.

And something that I took from her.

I don't have a real chance with Roisin, because even though she's good at pretending, I know she hates me.

How could she not, after everything I've done?

Quietly, I get up out of the bed. I close the door to the bathroom, quietly getting into the shower. I don't want to scrub Roisin off of me, but I need to get myself together.

I need to figure out what the fuck to do.

When I get out, my phone is lit up. I open it, noting that there's an email from what looks like a spam account. I almost don't open it, until another one comes in right after from the same address.

Cautiously, hoping that every technological advance I've done on my phone works and that I don't have to worry about a virus coming through, I open the email.

Give me the fucking girl.

. . .

There's nothing else. Not in the first email.

The second one, however, makes my heart stop.

It's a picture of Roisin and me. It's from the train station on the way to Italy, but it's recent enough that it makes my nerves go into overdrive.

It's also security camera footage. Meaning they either own the camera, or they hacked it, and either way, it sends a clear message.

Whoever the fuck this is, they can follow us. Monitor us.

And we have no idea how.

A third email pops up, and I click on it instantly. It's a coordinate, and when I click on it, it brings me to an address.

In Vienna.

Ice creeps down my spine.

Vienna is somewhat of a no-man's land when it comes to my world. It's a semi-neutral place, with its own families that run the crime scene, but it's an uneasy truce that keeps a balance. It's where a lot of the Eastern European families and the rest of us can find some common ground, because the city's own gangs are protective of the space, to the point where they don't allow any unsanctioned business.

Which means that whoever this is, they either know that...

Or they're to blame.

I fire off a quick text to Sal, just asking him who we know in Vienna. He quickly tries to video chat me, and I ignore the call.

Roisin is still asleep.

I can't wake her.

The second I do, the illusion will be over.

We need to stay together, for this. For now. Because the safety she has as my wife will buy her some time.

But after that?

I have to find a way to divorce her. I love her.

I love her far too much to shackle her to me for the rest of her life.

Sal calls me again, and this time, I take it. I'm walking around outside, pacing, as the nice Italian couple who owns the place cooks us breakfast. They made a big deal about us being newlyweds, a lie that flowed very easily when we checked in last night.

A lie that tastes like ash now.

"We don't know anyone in Vienna. What the fuck are you doing?" he barks.

"None of your business."

I can practically feel Sal's irritation. "Marco..."

"Who could possibly know anyone in Vienna?"

Sal huffs out a breath. "I don't know, man. I really fuckin' don't."

"I need to know."

"Because of your new girl?"

I freeze.

Seemingly sensing my reaction, Sal makes a noise. "You're trying to fix her life for her."

"I'm not."

"Liam told on you."

Fucking Liam. "I'm fine, Sal."

"It wouldn't fucking kill you to ask for help, goddamnit."

I pause.

Sal almost never curses at me.

He heaves a breath on the phone. "You're doing too much, man. You're all over the fucking place. And I know why you did it for us, I really do. But if you want to help your girl, you're going to need help yourself. You can't watch out for her without someone watching out for you. Trust me, I know."

I snort. "Do you?"

"Yeah, motherfucker. I had you watching out for me the whole time, remember?"

My heart pulses.

"All I'm saying," Sal continues, "is that you have done this for all of us. Me. Elio. Dino. You kind of helped Elio and Caterina, anyway, but I wouldn't say that you helped her."

"No," I say hoarsely. "I fucked that one up."

"You got lucky on that one. But it's time for us to help you, Marco. You've done enough on your own. You love this girl, right?"

"Woman," I correct him. "Roisin is more than that. She's my..."

I hesitate.

There are things that you tell people, and you can't un-tell them. Truth that once you put it out there in the world, you make it real.

The fact that Roisin is my wife?

I want it to be real. But as of right now, it isn't. Sure, we got married, but her question from the night before still slithers into my brain.

Pretend.

"Roisin is important to me," I end up saying, finishing on a really fucking lame note.

Sal hesitates, clearly not buying it. "Whatever, fine. Roisin is important to you. And you're going to need us. She's being framed, right?"

"Elio told you, didn't he," I grumble.

"I'm literally his eyes and ears out here in the world, bro. He didn't have to tell me."

For one second, I think of the security footage. Could Sal have betrayed me?

No.

He wouldn't.

He's family.

And family doesn't do that shit.

"Anyway. Okay. I've got some eyes on the Russians, because with Stassi and Liam, they're being shady as fuck. But I have the feeling this goes deeper, man."

My senses hone in on Sal, and I step forward. I don't think anyone at the inn is listening, but just in case, I walk toward the road, past where our car is parked, and glance around.

"What are you saying?"

I can practically hear Sal's shrug. "I'm not sure. I just feel like this is deep. Old. Something that stinks of family secrets and things that we should have left buried."

"I still don't get where you're coming from."

"Just something that dad said, a really long time ago. He said that nothing brings up old fucking baggage like when you've packed all your shit neatly."

I snort. "And that makes you think this is old?"

"We dug into Dino's past, Marco. We dug into it, and we ripped open a big fucking scab, and we didn't do that easily. He and Marisol are happy, right, but still... there has to be some kind of consequence for bringing the Drakos name back to life."

I pause.

"There wasn't anything to bring back. His cousin—"

"Seems to be perfectly happy. Dino's dad is dead. The twin is dead. But that shit's all too neat for me."

I open my mouth to refute him, but I pause.

Sal's instincts are good. More than good. Better than mine.

Instead of telling him to fuck off, I nod. "Okay. If you think there's something, there's something."

Sal's voice is full of disbelief. "Really?"

"Really."

"Fuck, okay. I'm going to look into it. You just keep low with your girl, okay? I've got you."

Hearing my little brother reassure me with such confidence is...

Well.

Humbling, I guess.

But still, it's nice.

I take a deep breath. "Sal...I appreciate that."

"Anything for you, brother," he says roughly. "Now, before I get too fucking sappy on you—"

I don't hear the end of that sentence.

In a second, everything changes.

I see the flash first, for some reason. The edge of my vision seems to burst, and I have the absolutely absurd thought that I've been hit by lightning. Then, however, I realize that there's no fucking lightning.

Because with the sound of the explosion comes the shock wave.

My phone flies out of my hand, and my body is thrown backward. I'm scrambling to stand, my ears are ringing, and I feel something hit my back, the pain altered by the realization that my back is hot as fuck.

Holy shit.

What fucking exploded?

Then, I realize that it's the inn.

I turn, and see that the entire west side of it is blown open. There's a gaping hole there, in the opposite corner from where Roisin and I were staying.

Roisin.

I stagger to my feet, trying to move forward. The innkeeper and his wife emerge, coughing, and I push past them.

Roisin is in the fucking burning building.

And I don't have a single thought in my head, except fucking finding her.

The site of the explosion is on fire now. Thick smoke fills the bottom floor, and I know that this is probably not structurally sound.

But I don't care.

I stumble up the stairs, my fingers reaching for the doorknob before I get up there. I move into the room, gasping.

Roisin.

The room is empty.

The bed is empty.

I rip it apart.

Everything is overturned. Everything is ripped apart. It takes me a solid five minutes, and the heat of the fire, before I realize something.

Roisin isn't here.

The explosion was a distraction.

I fucking fell for it.

And she's gone.

23

ROISIN

Waking up feels like I have the absolute worst hangover of all time.

My brain, at the moment, is made of complete and total mush. I have absolutely no idea where I am, which is strange. I can't remember the last time that I drank anything that would result in this level of hangover, actually.

Which is my first clue that something is very fucking wrong.

My second, of course, is when I realize that my arms and legs are tied.

And that the wooly feeling in my mouth is not a horrible case of bad breath...

But a gag, potentially of actual wool.

Fuck.

My first instinct is to panic, but I quickly fight against it. I've been trained for this. Whether it's living with my family or the training I've done with Interpol, I know how to get control of my emotions.

So I try that.

I take a breath. Then another. The binds on my wrist and ankles feel like plastic zip ties, and it's going to take a while to get out of them.

When I open my eyes, it's dark. Dark enough that I feel like I might be inside something. The low hum that I'm finally tuning into confirms that yes, I'm inside a moving vehicle.

Which is even fucking worse.

For a second, my mind goes to Marco. Did he do this? Did we have some kind of wonderful sex and then he just... kidnapped me?

My chest feels like it's going to cave in.

I have to consider the possibility. Logically, that's what makes sense.

But it's absolutely killing me to think that might be the case.

Not Marco.

But it could be Marco...

There's a jolt, and we come to a stop.

I think I might be in the trunk of a car.

There's a heart-stopping moment when I hear a key in the lock, and when it opens, I almost sag with relief to not see Marco there.

However, I tense again as rough hands haul me upwards.

"Well, you're a bit of a rough looking bird then aren't you?"

The voice is attached to an older man, and while the cadence reminds me of the British Isles, it's heavily accented. My vision is still a little blurry, but I can see that he's tall, with hair that's silver now but must have been dark and thick once.

His eyes are brown, his skin is darkly tanned, and a wicked scar crosses the entirety of his face.

Also, did he call me 'rough'?

If I didn't have a gag in my mouth, I'd spit on him.

He jerks me roughly forward, and I brace, expecting cold air. The early morning light, and subsequent air, however, is cool but not terrible. Clearly, we're not high in the Italian Alps anymore.

But that seems like a really big problem.

How did I get here, when I fell asleep in Marco's arms just moments ago. Or so it seems.

That's all I remember, anyway.

He pulls me forward, then leans down to cut the bonds on my ankles, and I grunt, a fissure of pain shooting through me as I go. I'm desperately trying to figure out where I am and what's going on as he tugs me forward.

All I can come up with is that I'm on the outskirts of some big city, and it's... big.

The signs nearby look like they're in German. I don't think we're in Germany though. The last time I was in Germany everything just felt... grey.

He drags me down toward a warehouse. I know instinctively that I can't get into that warehouse. I just can't do it.

If I do, bad things will happen.

So, I pull a classic move and I…

Flop.

Dead weight is always a good way to make sure that someone isn't going to have an easy time with you.

The man curses, in a language that sounds like… Greek?

Greek.

"Get up," he snaps at me.

I hold my hands up, letting my eyes water like I'm in pain. Like I'm someone who can't fight for myself.

If he comes closer, and I'm on the ground, I can use his weight to pull him down…

He leans in. *Yes.*

Even with my hands bound, I grab him and fling him onto the ground, using my body to pull myself up.

The man grunts, but I'm up. My hands might be bound but I'm running forward, and I duck into an alley.

The man is close behind me. In the pre-dawn light, it's easy to find me, so I keep going.

Streets weave past me, and I don't know where I am. I'm blindly charging forward, until I spot something…

There.

A shop.

I'm almost there. Feet away. When something hits me.

Greek cursing again. I'm quite sure that he's calling me a bitch, but I don't care.

I'm not going to die like this.

I fight like a cat, scratching with my nails and kicking aimlessly. The man roars at me, and I keep going. If he's hurt, it's working.

I'm almost free. Almost...

The crack of a gun makes both of us freeze.

"Let her go."

The voice is familiar, and while the man has his hand around my neck, he drags me up and holds me in front of him like a shield.

I turn, slowly, looking at the one person I'm so happy to see I could cry.

Marco.

He's holding a gun. He looks like he hasn't slept, his hair is wild, and he's staring at us with so much emotion in his eyes, I don't doubt for a second how he feels about me.

Marco loves me.

The realization washes over me. Every doubt I've had up until this moment feels like it doesn't matter.

Marco *loves me.*

I need to get the hell out of here so I can tell him that I love him too.

"Who the fuck are you?" Marco snarls.

The man laughs. "You look so much like him."

"I don't know who I look like, but if you don't let her go, I'm going to fucking blow a hole in your head," Marco snaps.

The man shuffles. "You talk like him too. Your father."

Marco blinks. "What about my father?"

"He took what's mine. Took something that belongs to me. So now I'm taking something of yours."

"My father's dead," Marco intones.

The man shuffles. He's breathing hard. That makes me think that I either landed a blow or...

Or Marco shot him.

"Unfortunate," the man says hollowly. "And even more so that you decided to give what should be mine to my son, because now I have two grudges to hold, against two De Lucas. One might be dead, but you?" I feel him shift, twisting my arm. "You're very much alive, and so is she."

"Touch my wife again and I'll fucking kill you," Marco snaps.

I can't pretend the words don't send a thrill through me. But, now isn't the time.

I need to get out of here.

I shuffle slightly, hoping Marco notices. If I flop again, the man might fall for it...

Marco's eyes catch mine, and I see him nod.

No matter what, he trusts me, and we're going to get through this, because I fucking love him.

And I won't die now.

"Your wife?" the man sneers. "Your mother was supposed to be my wife. She..."

That's enough.

I drop, and at the same moment, Marco fires.

The gunshot lands. I know because the man collapses behind me with a very gross, meaty sound. Seconds later, Marco's hands surround me, and he's tugging me into his chest.

"Roisin," he breathes. "My god, fuck, are you okay?"

I make a noise around the gag.

With shaking hands, he takes the gag off of me, and I breathe. "I'm fine," I whisper, hoarsely. "What the hell happened?"

"He took you from the inn. Must have hit you with some kind of a tranquilizer, and then took off from an airfield nearby. He blew up the inn—"

"The inn? Oh my god, is everyone okay?"

Marco nods. "Yeah. Amazingly, no casualties, but I was outside on the phone when the bomb went off."

"Jesus Marco," I breathe. I go to move my hands to touch his face, but they're still bound. "And you just what, hopped a plane?"

"Yeah," he murmurs.

I shake my head as Marco takes his knife to the plastic on my wrists, freeing me. "How did you find me?"

"Sal," he says softly. "Sal suspected that Dino's father took you… and he was right."

"Dino's father?"

Marco nods. "Dino's father kidnapped our mother, right after I was born. Dad raised Dino as his son, but the whole thing got really fucked up. Turns out Drakos was behind all of this.

Framing you, to come for me. He wanted revenge on the De Lucas, and he decided to take it... on me."

He helps me to my feet, and I'm about to say something, but I get wrapped into Marco's arms instead.

He holds me.

I hold him.

And in the space between heartbeats, I feel...

Better.

"I thought I lost you," Marco murmurs.

I make a noise.

"I thought I lost you, Roisin, and I can't... I never..."

"I love you," I blurt, pulling back.

Marco stares at me.

"I love you. I think we probably fucked this up, getting married like we did, but Marco... I don't want this to end. I'm sorry for everything, I know I'm not the best... I know that I come with a ton of baggage, but I love you," I whisper. "I'm scared as hell to tell you this, but I will anyway, because life is damn short and I..."

My torrent of words is cut off as Marco presses his lips to mine.

It's more than just a kiss. It's everything that we haven't said. Everything that we want to say. Everything that I've been meaning to tell him for months, ever since our time together in the little cottage on the Irish coast.

When the kiss breaks, I'm panting. I stare up at Marco.

He looks down at me, his lips tilted into a smile.

"I love you, Roisin," he murmurs.

Then, he gets down on one knee.

I blink. "Marco, what are you..."

"Roisin. I want you. I want this. I want us. I want to be a family with you now, forever, and always. Will you do the honor of marrying me?"

I shake my head. "Marco, we're already married."

He tilts his eyes to look at me, and the sincerity I see there makes my heart feel like it's squeezing itself.

"I didn't give you a choice before. I am now. Marry me. Please. Because I love you and I can't spend another day without you."

I mean. What's a girl to say to that?

I should let him worry, just a little. After all, poking at Marco's carefully formed boundaries is one of my favorite hobbies.

But I can't stop the smile that crosses my face.

Nor can I help the joy that I feel.

I kneel down to be on his level, placing my hands on either side of his face.

"I love you too, Marco De Luca."

"So you'll marry me," he tilts his head.

I lean in, then breathe one word against his lips.

"Yes."

EPILOGUE: ROISIN

ONE YEAR LATER

"We have to pack," I murmur.

Marco's lips trace over my shoulder. We're supposed to go on a cruise, to Antarctica, of all places. Traveling together has been the majority of this past year, and I couldn't be happier.

It's been a great way for Marco to disconnect from his family. For me to figure out who I am, and what I want.

And, for us to spend time together.

"I don't want to pack," Marco whispers against my skin.

I gently push him off me. I'm reluctant to do so, of course. Looking at Marco in the dim candlelight of our little cottage on the Irish coast, he looks like some kind of primal god. His skin is sculpted from the most perfect marble, and I can trace freckles over his perfect chest.

He growls as I look at him. "You don't want to pack either."

"I don't," I whisper, tracing the line of his perfect abs. "But we need to."

EPILOGUE: ROISIN

He sighs, kissing me before rolling off of me. "Fine," he stretches, and I take a minute to admire his ass. "You start the laundry, and I'll get the suitcases."

"Rude!" I call after him as he wanders into the bathroom.

I smile though, as I roll over.

This past year has been incredible.

We've seen every continent. Antarctica is the last one. We've been the best aunt and uncle to Marco's multitude of nieces and nephews. I've gotten to know Caterina and Gia and Marisol, and I'm absolutely in love with my new sisters.

And Stassi. Oh, Stassi. We've spent more than a few nights having girls' nights and stressing our guys out, but what can you do?

It's fun. Just plain fun.

And it's the family that I always wanted.

From the bathroom, I hear Marco make a noise. It's unusual, and I frown. I pull on my robe and stand, trotting in. "Marco?"

He turns, still naked, and when I see what's in his hands, I freeze.

"Were you planning on telling me about this?" he says roughly.

The positive pregnancy test in his hands is practically shaking in his grip.

I flush. I took the test earlier today, and I was planning on telling him. After we got on the cruise. Because if I know one thing about Marco, it's that the sight of those little pink lines is going to send him into full overdrive.

EPILOGUE: ROISIN

"Marco…"

"Cancel the trip," he growls.

I throw my hands up. "I was going to tell you!"

"When?"

"When we got there!"

"Roisin…"

I sigh and move forward, snatching the test out of his hands. "Marco. Seriously. We're going to be fine. We should just go."

"No."

"Fine. I'll go without you."

"Roisin…"

I stalk away.

Marco follows after, swooping me up. I snort, a little mad, but mostly melting into his arms.

He nuzzles my ear. "I don't want to put you at risk."

"You won't."

"Roisin…"

I spin, looking at him. "We're going to be parents," I smile at him. "And we're bringing a kid into a world where they are going to need all our skills to navigate it. You can't protect them, Marco. You have to let them learn to handle it."

His eyes search mine, and I cup the side of his face.

"You didn't want your family to feel sad, or hurt. Our baby is no different. And the lesson you learned from them?"

He shuts his eyes. "They don't need me to protect them."

EPILOGUE: ROISIN

"Well. The baby will. But you're a better teacher than protector, my love. Let's take them on all our adventures. Show them how to be the best version of us. How about that instead?"

He wrinkles his nose. "You just want to see penguins."

"I do want to see penguins. But we're going to do this," I murmur, putting his hand on my belly. "Just like we do everything. As a team."

He sighs, then kisses my lips. "I love you."

"I love you too."

"Are you sure?"

I laugh. "Come on, Marco. Let's pack."

We move around each other, and I smile.

I love adventures with Marco. I love the life we have.

And I can't wait for the adventures to come.

Thank you so much for reading my book, please leave me a review they help me succeed.

I'm in the throws of writing Liam and Stassi's book, follow me on Amazon to stay updated on when it will be on pre-order.

If you enjoyed Roisin and Marco you will love Gwen and Nikolai Petrov in Bratva King's Secret Twins

Here is a sneak peek...

Chapter 1

Gwen

EPILOGUE: ROISIN

"Well goddamn, darlin', you keep spinning like that you might just take my whole paycheck," Jacob, a regular with graying hair and a worn smile, yells to me.

I roll my hips, arching my back while I slide down the pole. My black curls cascade over my shoulder, and a sultry smile spreads across my lips.

"Baby," I purr, swinging my hair over my shoulder. I slide to the floor and crawl closer to the balding man holding a wad of 5's, "it'll be the best check you've ever spent."

He howls like a maniac, and his friends happily shower me with bills. *That's right, keep them coming. Your paycheck will definitely put me ahead of payments for Mason.*

I lean back, letting the pink light from above wash over me. The music fades, and Justin's sorry-ass voice comes over the loudspeaker. "Give it up for the delicious Cinnamon!" I roll back on my heels, licking my lips at the older men. "But hold onto your bulges, boys, because next up is a sweet little slice of heaven. Welcome Angel!"

I gather all the money I can, stuffing it into my panties and bra and make my way off the stage. "What the fuck, Dylan? I had at least ten more minutes in my set!"

Dylan, the club's owner, rolls his eyes as he lights a cigarette. "Gwen, you were boring the crowd."

"How fucking dare you—"

"Aye, watch your fucking mouth, or I'll take you off the books for a week!" I press my lips firmly together, crossing my arms over my chest.

"That's illegal, you know."

EPILOGUE: ROISIN

"And *you* know I don't like legal chat in my club." Dylan flicks the cigarette ash on the floor, giving me an annoyed look.

I smile, grabbing the cig out of his hand. "I see. I can only talk legalese when I'm getting you out of trouble." Dylan gives me a humorless laugh as I take a long pull. "Go figure."

Two years ago, I was at the top of my class at Georgetown Law, with dreams of becoming the best defense attorney in Washington, D.C. But then Dad disappeared after Mason threatened to break his legs. Mason had told Nana Rose that Dad's debt was her debt. Despite everyone telling me not to, I dropped out of Law School to help pay off the debt because no one hurts Nana Rose, not if I can help it.

So when Dylan's club was facing the threat of being shut down due to rumors of illegal activities in the secret "peek-a-boo" rooms upstairs, we made a deal: I would use my legal expertise to help him, and in return, he would allow me to work on the main stage at Dream Palace until I paid off my father's debt.

"Ha. Ha. Funny." Dylan snatches his cigarette back. "Now go out there and offer a dance to some of Mason's crew. They haven't spent any money yet."

Fuck. I shift my weight from side to side, biting the inside of my cheek. Mason probably sent some of his men to collect the measly 500 dollars I pay towards my father's quarter of a million-dollar debt. "Come on, they love Angel way more than me." I roll my eyes, trying to count the bills in my hands quickly.

"Chop. Chop. You know you're Tyler's favorite." I roll my eyes, continuing to count. 15. 20. 25. Fuck, I only got 375.

EPILOGUE: ROISIN

I push my breasts up and take a deep breath, steeling my nerves. "I thought I was boring," I mock, sticking my tongue out at Dylan.

"Don't pick a fight with me. Get out there." Dylan points the cigarette at the door behind me, and I huff, sharply turning around on my six-inch stilettos.

I add an extra sway in my hips and make my way to the main floor, sliding just out of reach of some of the handsy men. I get wolf calls and "Hey baby," but there is one set of eyes that silently weigh on me.

I look up to the left corner of the club, my eyes locking with a set of deep blue eyes. His gaze burns into mine, causing a thrill to ripple through me. I can feel his eyes tracing every curve, every dip of my silhouette, as I make my way through the club. I am drowning in his bright blue eyes.

He holds my gaze and lazily sips the amber liquid from his tumbler. I lean forward, eyes hooded behind the rogue strand from his slick back, dirty blonde hair. I can't help but keep my gaze on him, his presence drawing me like a moth to a flame.

"Goddamn, you are fine!" Tyler's whistle breaks the man's trance. I look up at the smug motherfucker in a white tank top and dirty blue jeans. His buzz cut is colored green but looks purple under the neon lights, and despite all the ways he could be cute, he is just shy of being good-looking.

I stare at the angry pink scar pulsating on his face, but I mask the shiver of disgust with a seductive smile. "Well, I heard you boys were looking for me?"

"Hell yeah, baby!" An eager member who looks a little too young to be in here smiles, looking at the rose tattoo that spirals up my legs and gathers on my left butt cheek.

EPILOGUE: ROISIN

"Come sit on Daddy's lap, Gwen." There is nothing more unattractive than a man calling himself Daddy. Major ick. That honor should be bestowed upon you, not self-titled.

"Oh, come, Ty. If you want to take me home, you need to try harder than that." I walk closer, almost between his thighs, crossing one foot in front of another, sliding my hips side to side like a snake charmer. Tyler leans back in his chair, legs wide, eyes hooded with a visible tent growing in his jeans.

"You know Mason won't let none of us touch you." I give him my best pout, squatting between his legs and peering up through my eyelashes.

Leaning up by his ear, I whisper, "Well, ain't that too damn bad." I'm not fucking Mason. I'm not fucking anyone, never have, but Mason claimed me as if I was his future wife. He knows if I had it my way, I'd have him swimming with the fishes before I would ever voluntarily call him husband.

Tyler swallows, his eyes running over the curves of my body. When his eyes land on mine, he licks his lips and says, "Jordan is waiting outside for this week's payment. Side door."

"Thanks, love." I wink, blowing Tyler a kiss that makes his eyes lower.

With a flamboyant flourish, I turn around and switch my hips over to the side door when my eyes drift up to that man again. The tumbler he was drinking out of is abandoned on the side table next to his empty seat, glittering under the dance lights. I huff, blowing air between my lips. You need to get it together, Gwen; no paying attention to the hot, mysterious stranger's absence when Venom is waiting for payment.

Maneuvering through the crowd and keeping out of Dylan's eyeline, I make my way to the side alley. Knocking my right

EPILOGUE: ROISIN

shoulder into the metal door, I stumble into the side alley where the midnight air bites at my exposed flesh. I gaze to my right, where Venom lazily smokes a cigarette.

"Venom, buddy!" I laugh, holding the metal door open with my hip and crossing my arms under my chest. "How the hell are ya?"

Venom, a big, burly man with thin lips and a bald head so shiny it gleams in the streetlights, smiles at me, flicking the ash from the cigarette at my feet. "Well, Gwendolyn—"

"Ew, not my full government." I grimace. Venom smirks, looking at me from the corner of his eye, and if I didn't watch him break my father's kneecap with his bare hands, Venom would be just my type. He is the enforcer in Mason's inner circle, and if I ever stopped paying my payments, Venom would be the one to track me down and kill me after he has all the fun he wants with me, and from his gaze, I can tell I would be in for a long night.

"From the tone of your voice," he takes another pull of his cigarette, "you're missing part of your payment." I cross my legs, giving my most innocent smile.

"Oh, only by 125 dollars."

Venom lets out a low whistle.

"But I have three hours left in this shift. I promise I'll have it by the end. I mean, come look at these." I motion to my breasts with a clever grin on my face.

Venom finally turns his body to me, his eyes shamelessly ogling my chest. His smile widens, showcasing his pearly whites, while his eyes move from my breasts to the curve created by my tiny waist and wide hips.

EPILOGUE: ROISIN

I place my left hand on my hip. "Woah there, Venom. Keep looking at me like that, and I'll charge you."

Venom tosses the cigarette on the floor and places both of his large hands on my hips, dragging me into his chest. I yelp, scrambling to fight him off before the door closes, but I am too late, and he is too strong. "You know there is an easier way to work off that debt, Gwen."

"Oh," I giggle nervously, trying to wiggle out of his embrace, but Venom pulls me in closer, forcing me to inhale his stink of cigarettes. I almost gag on the smoke still spilling out of his lips. I make my voice firm, losing all of my playfulness as I make eye contact with his black eyes. "Venom, if you are looking for a lap dance, go inside the club."

"Baby, I don't want no fucking lap dance," Venom's smile is sinister, "I want you on your knees sucking my dick," he whispers heavily.

"Venom, what the fuck?" I jerk back in his arms, moving to knee him in the dick.

"You're right; that's only worth like fifty." His hands run from my waist, and he grips both of my cheeks, kneading my ass. "I'll fuck you in the ass after. We can call that an even 200, what do you say?"

"Mason will fucking kill you-"

"Nah, because you are going to be a good girl and not say a word." He pulls me in closer and licks my cheek.

"Venom, you bring your dick anywhere near me and I'll bite it off," I growl, slamming the heel of my stilettos into the toe of his combat boots; he doesn't even flinch.

EPILOGUE: ROISIN

"I always knew fucking you would be rough." Venom spins me around, wrapping my hair around his hand. He tries to push me down to my knees.

No. No. No. I can't lose my virginity like this and definitely not to a guy named fucking Venom. I dig my heels into the ground, using my body as leverage to keep me from hitting the ground, but Venom is too strong. My knees buckle, and I am left panting and praying to Gods I don't believe in for any solace.

A shot whizzes through the air. Venom jumps back, looking for his weapon, and tosses me to the ground as if I am nothing. "Fucking hell," Venom growls, searching the area for the assailant.

"I don't miss twice." A thick Russian accent rumbles through the air, but I am in too much panic to appreciate it.

The minute I hit the ground, I pat the area around me, looking for a weapon to defend myself. My fingers wrap around the neck of an empty beer bottle. I grab it, smashing it against the concrete wall and stumbling over to the other side of the alley, out of Venom's reach, brandishing the broken bottle as a weapon.

"When a lady says no, the answer is no." The silky tenor of the voice causes a shiver to run down my spine. My eyes lock with the same bright blue eyes I almost drowned in.

Chapter 2

Gwen

With bright blue eyes, a man emerges from the shadow of the alley, caressing the pipe of his pistol as if it were a loyal dog.

EPILOGUE: ROISIN

Venom sneers, "You better fuck off before Mason has your fucking head."

Blue Eyes's lips spread into a sinister smile as if he was a kid playing with his favorite toy. "Oh, and this Mason lets you run around and rape young women?"

"Mason owns this city and everyone in it." Venom laughs as he points to me. "Especially her, so I'd mind my fucking business if I were you."

Blue Eyes shrugs. "You see, I would if she didn't say no, and well-" He winks at me. "When a beautiful girl says no to a jackass like you, I can't help myself."

It all happens in a flash. Blue Eyes reaches for Venom's gun, twisting his body so Venom's head is on the sidewalk, underneath Blue Eyes's knee, and his arm bent back so that Blue Eyes could easily break his arm.

Underneath the streetlight, I can see his slick back, dirty blonde hair, with a rogue strand dancing above his right eye, which is brown. I want to tuck that strand back so it can spring back and have a reason to touch him again. His blue eyes are vibrant and deep like the ocean, and he has swirls of intricate black tattoos peeking out of his button-up and up his neck. I swallow as my eyes land on the vein popping on the forearm that stretches to put pressure on Venom's shoulder blade.

When he looks up at me, there is a sparkle in his eye, and his lips are in an easygoing smile. "Normally, I'd break your arm, but since you were bothering the lady, I think it's only right that it is her choice what we do with you."

I twist my lips as if I am in deep thought because the idea of Blue Eyes breaking Venom's arm for me makes my panties

EPILOGUE: ROISIN

wet. "Well, before you break anything in my honor, how about you tell me your name?" I purr, leaning forward to his eye level. Venom struggles beneath him, a slew of curses leaving his lips.

He brandishes a bright smile, rolling his name off his tongue like we are meeting in line at a coffee shop. "Nikolai Petrov, pleasure."

"Nikolai? Petrov?" Venom whimpers.

"In the flesh." Nikolai's cocky smile flashes in my direction with a flourish.

"Petrov, wait, I-I-" Venom begins to beg, but Nikolai clicks his tongue, silencing him.

"No. No begging now." Nikolai twists his arm, causing Venom to yelp, but he brings his eyes back to me. "Our handsy friend is getting a little impatient..."

"Gwen. I would shake your hand, but they seem full right now." I smile, flipping my curls over my shoulder, the broken bottle still swinging between my fingertips.

"Well, *Gwen.*" *Fuck, I love the way he pours over my name.* "What would you like me to do with the handsy guy here?"

"Hmmm, you see, a broken arm can heal."

"Continue." Nikolai nods, intrigue flashing across his eyes as a devilish smile spreads.

"And I think this fucker needs a permanent reminder to keep his hands to himself." I purse my lips as if contemplating before looking down into Venom's eyes. "Don't ya' think, Venny?"

"Gwen, I swear to God-"

EPILOGUE: ROISIN

"Threaten her, and I will take your tongue as a souvenir," Nikolai growls, and heat rushes straight to my core. "Continue, love."

"Thank you." I beam. "I vote for a pinky finger, not too significant, but he'll miss it."

"I like the way you think, Kotik." Nikolai pulls a knife out of his back pocket, flipping it open. He looks at the hand he is currently twisting away from Venom's body, pressing the knife to the base of his pinky. He looks down at Venom with a nasty grin. "This may hurt a tad bit, mate."

The alleyway fills with the screams of Venom, and I think I am in love with a psycho.

Venom shakes in the fetal position, vibrating from the pain as he holds his bleeding hand. Nikolai looks at me with a mischievous smile, with the pinky in his hand. "For you, Kotik."

"How romantic," I deadpan. "Normally, men get me diamonds and dinner first."

Nikolai throws the pinky away as far from Venom as possible. "Those men are carbon copies of each other. At least you will remember my name," he teases.

A smirk dances on my face. I cross my right arm under my chest and placing an inquisitive finger on my chin. "I'm sorry, what's your name again?"

He laughs in his low voice as he grabs my hand, kisses it, and whispers, "My name is yours if you want it to be."

My cheeks heat up, and electricity sparks where his lips connect with my skin. There is no reason for one man to be so sexy and smooth with eyes that make me so weak in the knees.

EPILOGUE: ROISIN

The smirk he gives me while he looks at me through his eyelashes will end me.

"Jeez, you're too much of a charmer for your own good."

The laughter that rumbles through his chest causes me to catch my breath, wishing to hear the sound again and again. "And you are too beautiful for your own good. A girl like you should be throwing the tips, not dancing for them."

I pop my hip to the right, my nails wrapping around my hip. "What? You didn't like my dancing?"

Nikolai's eyes heat, his tongue poking out to brush over his lower lip before poking his inner left cheek and looking away.

"Oh my God, do you think I am a bad dancer?"

Nikolai's hand loops around my waist, his hand spreading over my lower back, pulling me into his chest. The motion startles me and I drop the beer bottle. The scent of leather and fresh rain invades my senses. His eyes flutter to my lips, the boyish smirk spreading across his lips before he makes eye contact with my breathless body. "No, my love, I love your dancing." His voice lowers. "I just would rather you do it in private for me."

I can't breathe. I can't think, not with Nikolai this close, and for the first time since the fourth grade, I fucking stutter. "W-well, i-if you wanted a d-dance. All you had to do was ask." *Jesus. Fuck. Get it together, Gwendolyn.*

His nose grazes mine. "Dance for me."

"When?" He slides his phone into my hand.

"Tomorrow. Let me take you out and show you the lifestyle you're supposed to be living." My mouth parts mindlessly, and

EPILOGUE: ROISIN

I gather all the shallow breaths I possibly can as I type my number into his phone.

"Pick me up at 8," I say. Nikolai lets me go, and I immediately feel the chill of the night consume me.

He winks at me, not even checking if I gave him my real number, the cocky bastard.

Continue reading Gwen and Nikolai's story Bratva King's Secret Twins now available on Amazon, Free with Kindle unlimited, and available on paperback.

ABOUT THE AUTHOR

Vivy Skys writes addictive high heat romance where grumpy, dangerously hot alpha males fall hard for sassy, stunning women who bring them to their knees.

From billionaires in penthouse suites to irresistible neighbors next door—and let's not forget the wickedly charming royals, protective SEALs and Mafia Kings—no swoon-worthy bachelor is safe.

Vivy's heroines are clever, confident, and impossible to forget—exactly the kind of women these men would burn kingdoms to worship.

Each scorching, standalone love story promises heart-pounding tension, heat you'll feel in your bones, and the kind of happily-ever-after that'll leave you breathless.

🔥 Ready to get obsessed? Dive into the Vivy's Library—and don't forget to join her raving fan newsletter for sneak peeks, bonus books, and insider-only treats

[Follow Vivy Skys on Amazon](#) to be the first to know when her next book becomes available.